MONTANA SEAL DADDY
BROTHERHOOD PROTECTORS

BOOK #7

ELLE JAMES

New York Times & *USA Today*
Bestselling Author

Dedication

This story is dedicated to my family who has been there for me, encouraged me and shown me so much love my heart is full and happy. Thank you for being there. I love you all so very much.

Elle James

About This Book

*Former Navy SEAL enters the fight of his life to
protect the mother of his child from killers who wish to
silence her testimony in a murder case.*

After the sudden disappearance of the
amazing woman he fell for on vacation in
Cozumel, and then nearly losing his own life on a
politically volatile mission in Syria, Brandon
Rayne "Boomer" leaves the SEAL brotherhood
and signs on with the private security agency
Brotherhood Protectors in Montana. Determined
to forget the girl and maybe even try for a real
life and start a family, he embraces his new life.

While on vacation in Cozumel, Daphne
Miller fell in love with a hunky SEAL. On the
verge of committing her heart and life to him,
she becomes the unwitting witness to murder.
Forced into witness protection, she doesn't
realize she's pregnant, the product of the hot
fling with the sexy SEAL. A year later, still pining
for what could have been, with a baby girl to
protect, Daphne's safe house is compromised. In
an attempt to evade the people trying to kill her
to keep her from being a star witness in a big
court case, she heads to Montana to find the only
person she knows can help, the baby's father.

Determined to put his desire for Daphne on
the back burner, Boomer focuses his skills and

cunning on keeping her alive long enough to testify. Together, they vow to protect baby Maya from becoming collateral damage by Daphne's would-be assassins.

Author's Note

If you enjoy reading about military heroes, read
other books in Elle James's
Brotherhood Protector Series:

Montana SEAL (#1)
Bride Protector SEAL (#2)
Montana D-Force (#3)
Cowboy D-Force (#4)
Montana Ranger (#5)
Montana Dog Soldier (#6)
Montana SEAL Daddy (#7)
Montana Rescue (#8)

Visit www.ellejames.com for more titles and
release dates
For hot cowboys, visit her alter ego
Myla Jackson at www.mylajackson.com

Chapter 1

"I don't think I'll ever get used to this heat." Daphne Miller sat on the front porch of the small clapboard house out in the middle of the hills in practically nowhere Utah. She fanned herself with a five-month old copy of a celebrity magazine, wishing she were anywhere else in the world. "Do you think they're any closer to getting the evidence they need to nail the bastard who killed Sylvia Jansen? I'd think my testimony alone would be sufficient to put him away for a very long time. Otherwise, why go to all the trouble of witness protection?"

Her forty-seven-year-old bodyguard with the gray streaks at his temples and weathered skin sat in a wooden rocking chair, his feet resting on the porch railing, a piece of straw sticking out of his mouth. Chuck Johnson rolled the straw between his teeth before answering. "You'd think after a year, the feds would have what they need."

Daphne pushed to her feet, restlessness fueling her irritation. "All I know is that I've sat in this cabin in this godforsaken heat for longer than I can stand. I need to move on with my life. I can't stay here forever. For all we know, they've forgotten I saw anything. Harrison Cooper probably thinks I'm dead or fell off the face of the earth. He might have moved on to his next victim by now. And I'm sitting here doing nothing." She paced to the end of the porch and back, skirting Chuck and his feet propped against the porch railing.

A tiny cry sounded inside the house.

"I'll get her." Chuck dropped his booted feet to the porch and hurried inside to check on Maya, Daphne's three-month old baby girl.

Daphne held up her hands and snorted. "He's even better at parenting than her own mother." She loved Maya, but sometimes she wondered if Maya loved Chuck more than her.

Chuck returned to the porch carrying Maya on one arm, cradling the back of her head with his opposite hand. He handed the child to Daphne. "I changed her, but it's not a dirty diaper that's making her fussy. She's hungry."

Daphne took the baby in her arms, sank into the rocking chair and lifted the hem of her tank top.

Too hot for a bra, she'd left it off that morning, giving Maya free access to her milk supply.

The baby rooted around until she found Daphne's nipple and sucked hungrily, making slurping noises that made Daphne laugh.

Chuck cleared his throat and turned away. "I'll make some iced tea."

"Thank you." Daphne smiled at the man's reluctance to watch the baby nursing. Hell, he'd been there when Maya was born and helped Daphne when she'd had trouble getting the baby to latch on. Why he would feel the need to give her privacy now was a mystery. But Daphne liked to push his buttons. Anything for a reaction in the incredible boredom of her current situation.

Short of feeding Maya, Chuck did everything else with the baby, including getting down on the floor to play with her when Daphne was too tired to entertain her sweet baby girl.

How she wished things had turned out differently. But then she'd wished that for the past year. Not the part about being pregnant or having a baby. Maya was the light of her life. What Daphne despised was being stuck in this godforsaken corner of the Utah desert hill country with nothing to do but count the minutes of every day. If something didn't happen soon, she'd explode.

She switched Maya to the other breast and let the baby drink her fill. The day was much like every other day. Wake up to feed Maya, change her diaper, cook breakfast for herself and Chuck and, sometimes, one of the other guards. The sun rose, the sun set and on and on and on... Only the occasional rare, violent storm ever broke their routine. God, how she wished for one now.

Daphne leaned Maya up on her shoulder and patted the bubbles out of her tummy. She cradled the baby in the curve of her arm and then sat in the growing heat, wondering where she'd gone wrong in her life to deserve so much drama and yet so much boredom.

Chuck emerged through the back screen door and took up his position in the rocking chair. For all intents and purposes, he appeared to be relaxed and enjoying the suffocating heat of the late fall day.

Daphne sighed and rocked Maya in her arms. "I'll be glad when winter finally gets here."

"You and me both," Chuck said, his gaze on the horizon and his voice even.

"Tell me again about what you did for the Navy SEALs," Daphne coaxed.

In profile, he arched an eyebrow. "I already told you a dozen times. Aren't you tired of my stories?"

She shrugged. "Beats boredom. And it gives me an idea of what Maya's father might be doing right now, as we speak."

Chuck sighed. "There's nothing sexy about tromping through the desert, carrying all of your equipment on your back, steel plates in your vest and facing an enemy that uses women and children as shields to block the bullets meant for them."

Daphne stared down at Maya, her heart contracting. She couldn't imagine someone putting a bullet through her baby girl's chest. "Then tell me about your training to become a SEAL." She liked hearing about the rigors of BUD/S training, and how only the best of the best made it through to the end.

Chuck had survived BUD/S training. Since Brandon had made it through as well, he was another man who'd proved he was one of the best.

Again, Chuck sighed and started at the beginning of his training and told her of the different weeks and what each entailed.

Daphne half-listened...and half-daydreamed about meeting Maya's father in Cozumel.

She'd been there on what should have been her honeymoon, but had turned out to be a solitary vacation. She'd gone with a heavy heart, having lost her fiancé six months earlier to a brain tumor. Because they'd had non-refundable tickets, Jonah had insisted she go, even though it would be without him.

During his treatment and decline, Daphne had been at his side. He'd insisted she go as part of her promise to move on, find love, get married and have children.

At the time of Jonah's death, Daphne was convinced she'd never find another man to love as much as she'd loved Jonah. He'd been her everything, from the moment they'd met in high school, through college and during his final hours on earth.

He'd loved her unconditionally and had wanted half-a-dozen children with her, the little house with the white picket fence and everything normal couples dreamed of when making plans for their futures.

Two months after he'd proposed to her, he'd fallen ill. After many tests, X-rays, scans and MRIs, the diagnosis had been grim. He had terminal brain cancer and less than five months to live.

All of their plans were pushed to the side as they fought to change that diagnosis to something that involved growing old together.

Alas, nearly five months sped by, and no amount of medication slowed the growth of the tumor. At four months, three weeks and two days following his diagnosis, Jonah slipped into a coma and died in Daphne's arms.

Before he passed, he'd made her promise to go on their honeymoon and find a man who made her heart beat faster. A man who would love her always and provide her with the family she and Jonah had always wanted. And he'd asked her to name a little girl after their honeymoon resort in remembrance of the love Daphne and Jonah had shared in his short time on earth.

Daphne stared down at the baby girl in her arms.

Maya with her black curls, so unlike Daphne's straight blond hair. Jonah had had light brown hair and blue eyes. Nothing about Maya reminded Daphne of Jonah, except her name.

Even then, she reminded Daphne more of the man she'd met in Cozumel, her baby's father, a tall, dark, handsome Navy SEAL who'd found her sitting on the beach one night, alone and crying.

Brandon Rayne, or Boomer, as his teammates had nicknamed him, could have walked away, leaving the weepy woman on the sand in the moonlight, but he hadn't. He'd dropped down beside her, taken her hand, pulled her into his arms and held her until her tears stopped falling.

He'd listened to her sad story, patted her back and held her. When she'd wiped away the tears and collected herself, he'd stood, held out a hand and pulled her up into his arms and kissed her forehead. "Everything is going to be all right," he'd assured her.

She stared up into his moonlit dark eyes. "How do you know?"

He chuckled. "I don't. But being on a sandy beach with a beautiful woman makes me wholly optimistic." Then he'd walked her back to her room at the resort and given her his cell phone number in case she ever wanted to walk on the beach at night. He didn't like the idea of her walking alone.

And that's how their brief and fiery romance spun up into a raging flame. If Daphne believed in ghosts, she'd bet Jonah had sent the SEAL to remind her that her fiancé had died, not her. She had a life to live, and oh, by the way, this handsome SEAL seemed interested in her and wanted to spend time with her.

Once she got over the guilt, Daphne enjoyed the quiet walks at night on the beach. And what was moonlight without a kiss?

One kiss with Boomer wasn't nearly enough. By the second night, he'd invited her to dance and then to his bungalow for a drink. The remaining five days were spent together in paradise. Swimming, dancing, parasailing and learning how to love as if for the first time.

When the last night came, Daphne slipped out of his room, after he fell asleep to return to hers to pack for the trip home. She hadn't wanted to wake him, hating tearful goodbyes. She wanted to remember him as he was, big, gorgeous and naked against the sheets.

On her way from his bungalow to her room in the tower, she'd run across a young man, arguing with a woman.

The woman slapped the young man.

Daphne had been too far away to hear what she said, but clearly, she wasn't happy with the man. When the woman turned to walk away, the blond man clasped her wrist and spun her toward him.

She told him to let go.

When he didn't, she tugged hard, trying to free herself.

Daphne had sped up, trying to get closer to help the woman.

By the time she reached them, the blond man had wrapped his hands around the woman's neck so tightly, he was choking her.

The woman beat at his chest with her fists, but he wouldn't release his grip.

Daphne grabbed a stick from the ground and hit the man over and over, but he wouldn't let go of the woman until her body sagged and fell to the ground.

Then he turned his attention to Daphne.

The man blocked the path, preventing her from running back to the bungalow where Boomer lay sleeping peacefully.

With no other choice, Daphne spun and ran toward the resort, the sound of footsteps pounding on the path behind her. She'd almost reached the entrance when an arm reached out of the darkness, grabbed her, yanked her into the shadow of the bushes, and pushed her toward the ground. A hand clamped over her mouth, muffling her attempt to scream.

"Be still, or he'll find you and kill you," a voice whispered into her ear.

Steps crunched on the gravel path, heading her direction.

Daphne lay still, more afraid of the man who'd choked a woman to death than the stranger holding her in the darkness.

The killer stalked past her, his eyes narrow, his gaze darting into the shadows. In his left hand, he held a small handgun.

Freezing in place, Daphne held her breath, praying he didn't see her lying there. Vulnerable to the man holding her and to the killer brandishing a gun, she prayed she'd chosen the lesser of two evils.

The assailant tucked the weapon into waistband of his trousers and closed his suit jacket over the bulge, before entering the resort tower.

Not until the door closed behind him, did Daphne let go of the breath she'd held.

The man holding her removed his hand from her mouth and loosened the arm around her middle.

She scrambled to her feet and stared at the stranger as he pushed to his feet and stood. He towered over her, his muscular body even more proof he could have had his way with her and she'd have had little chance of fighting free.

That's how she remembered meeting Chuck.

He'd been the one responsible for saving her life and that of her unborn baby by whisking her away from Cozumel and back to the States.

"I'm Agent Johnson. Chuck Johnson." He'd shown her his credentials as a DEA agent in pursuit of a man who smuggled drugs and murdered beautiful women.

"That man chasing you happens to be the son of a high-powered senator. He's suspected of drug and human trafficking, as well as several counts of murder."

"Then why aren't you stopping him?" Daphne demanded.

"He's a slippery bastard. The witnesses or drug dealers have a habit of turning up dead before charges can be brought against him." The stranger frowned. "Why was he chasing you?"

Daphne's heart plummeted into her belly as she recalled how hard the woman had fought and how many times Daphne had hit the man with the stick to no avail. "He killed a woman."

"Show me." Chuck edged up to the path, glancing both ways before motioning for her to go ahead of him.

Before they reached the point at which the woman had been strangled, two men appeared from the direction of the beach, dressed in black. The glow of the Tiki lamps lighting the path glinted off the smooth metal of the pistols they carried in their hands.

Chuck pulled her back into the shadows and blocked her body with his.

But he didn't block her entire vision.

The two men in black moved the woman's body, carrying it toward the ocean.

"See what I mean?" her muscular rescuer said. "He has a cleanup detail following him around."

Shocked at what she'd just seen, Daphne tried to push him aside. "You can't let him get away with killing someone."

"And what do you suggest? If I kill those men, it will appear as if I killed the woman. You and I will be split up, and more cleanup crews will be called in to deal with you and me. Our best bet is to get you out of here before they come looking for you."

At that exact moment, two more men appeared, coming from the direction of the resort, also dressed in black and carrying weapons.

Daphne sank back into the bushes, shaking. "I know the man staying in the fourth bungalow from the end of the path. We can hide there," she suggested.

Chuck shook his head. "No good. If you were there before, they'll track you down to that location again. The staff knows the comings and goings of all the guests. And they can be bribed."

But Daphne wanted to go back to where she'd left Boomer sleeping. If she'd stayed with him the entire night, she wouldn't be in this predicament. The woman would still be dead, but Daphne wouldn't now be targeted for elimination.

Again, she stayed still, waiting for the two men in black to pass by their position. She had no other choice in the matter. She had to get away from the scene of the crime. Perhaps then, they could circle back and report the crime to the local authorities.

That had been a year ago.

As far as Daphne knew, Harrison Cooper was still free, while she and Maya had been stuck in a cabin in Utah, waiting for something to happen that would put Cooper behind bars.

When Chuck paused in his description of Hell Week at BUD/S, Daphne pushed to her feet. "I'm going to go put Maya to bed. Hold that thought. I want to hear more." She smiled at the only human contact she'd had besides the doctors and nurses who'd delivered her baby in the Salt Lake City hospital and her two-man protection crew who guarded the entrance to this lonely house.

Chuck had admitted he wasn't with the DEA. He was with a super-secret government entity, assigned to clean up corruption amongst politicians. He'd come up with false identification and insurance cards to cover her and the baby. As soon as she was able, he'd packed up her and Maya and orchestrated their disappearance from the hospital into the foothills of Utah's Wasatch Mountain Range, near the Wyoming border.

Daphne had grown to love Chuck like a surrogate father or a favorite big brother. On more than one occasion, she found herself referring to him as Maya's godfather. And he was her only link to the outside world.

He had connections with the SEAL community, having retired from the Navy before taking on a role with the DEA.

Daphne knew, if she asked, he'd tell her where Boomer was, and whether he was dead or alive. When she'd been at her lowest, suffering from postpartum depression shortly after Maya was born, he'd told her Boomer was back in the States, preparing to deploy to Iraq.

She'd been tempted to reach out to Boomer and let him know he had a beautiful baby girl. But how fair would that have been, knowing he was about to deploy. And by letting him know about his baby, she might give up her location, something she couldn't afford to do. Her life wasn't nearly as important to her as keeping Maya safe.

Now that she had a baby, she had to do

everything in her power to protect Maya from Harrison Cooper's cleanup team. As effective as they'd been in Cozumel, they would show no remorse over using an infant as a bargaining chip to lure Daphne out into the open. Once they located her, she'd disappear, and then they'd have no use for Maya.

Daphne's heart squeezed hard in her chest as she laid her baby in the crib.

Maya's sweet lips puckered as if she were still suckling at Daphne's breast. She squirmed, stretched and laid still, her belly full, her comfort secured.

Daphne smiled and straightened, her attention drawn to the window overlooking the dirt road leading up to the cabin. A plume of dust rose from a vehicle moving swiftly up the mile-long track.

A second of concern rippled through Daphne, but she refused to be alarmed. Not yet.

Their dayshift gate guard, Rodney Smith, was one of two men who'd been assigned to provide backup and support. Rodney was on day shift, while Paul Caney preferred nights and slept in town during the day. They stood guard at the entrance gate to the mountain cabin a mile away, keeping in contact with Chuck via handheld, two-way radios.

"Chuck? Has Rodney checked in?" she called out.

Chuck entered the house, passed the door to Maya's nursery and exited through the front door onto the porch. With the two-way radio held to his ear, his gaze fixed on the cloud of dust racing toward them. "Smith, report," he said over and over.

When nothing but static came across the radio, Chuck spun and raced back into the house, his face stern, his fists clenched. "Take Maya to the shed. Now! This isn't a drill."

Daphne's heart tripped and raced. They'd practiced this drill numerous times. If Chuck said take Maya to the shed, they were in trouble.

Daphne reached for her "go pack", the backpack carrying the essentials necessary for the baby, slung it over her shoulders, then she gathered Maya into her arms and ran out the back of the house to the shed.

In the shed, she pulled a baby sling over her shoulder, settled Maya into the sling and tightened it so that she fit snugly against Daphne's chest. She settled a helmet over her head and buckled the strap.

Chuck arrived a few seconds later and flung open the back doors he'd installed on the shed.

"Everything set?" Daphne asked as she swung her leg over the seat of a four-wheeler.

He nodded. "Do you want me to take Maya?"

Daphne shook her head. "I've got her."

"You can take the lead until we reach the pass. I've got your six. The paths are narrow. The vehicles coming up the road won't be able to follow for long—if they make it past the surprise

I left for them."

"Where will we go?" Daphne asked.

"I have a friend in Montana. He'll know what to do. He'll help protect you and Maya."

Daphne nodded, pressed the throttle lever on the four-wheeler and sent the vehicle lurching forward and up the trail into the mountains.

Chuck followed, bringing up the rear, armed to the teeth with rifles, handguns, knives and hand grenades.

All they had to do was get far enough away from rifle fire, and they'd make good their escape from those attacking the cabin. But the race up the side of the mountain left them exposed for several minutes. What they needed was a distraction.

Daphne didn't look back, she held tightly to the handlebars of the ATV, moving as quickly as she could up the rough mountain trail, praying the men heading for the cabin didn't stop and take aim at the riders on the escaping four-wheelers.

An explosion echoed off the hillsides, followed by another, even bigger, that ripped through the air, shaking the earth beneath the four, knobby tires. Daphne nearly lost her grip on the four-wheeler handlebars. She risked a quick glance over her shoulder at the cabin. Nothing remained of her temporary home. Nothing but debris, fire and smoke.

Chuck slowed, frowning. "I planned on the first explosion, but not the second."

"Did you detonate the house?" Daphne asked.

Her protector shook his head. "No. I had some trip wires set up in front of the house. Looks like it just made them mad enough to destroy the house."

Daphne swallowed the sob rising up her throat, threatening to choke off her air. That cabin had been her baby's first home. The crib, the extra clothing and toys had been all Maya had known. Where they'd go from here was a huge unknown.

All Daphne knew was she had to get Maya to safety. Everything that had been in the cabin was just *stuff*. She could replace stuff. She couldn't replace the life of her baby girl.

Chuck had a friend in Montana.

After a year, waiting for something to happen and thinking it never would, Daphne was now a believer. Her heart weighed heavily for the guard on the gate. More than likely, Rodney was dead.

She prayed Chuck's friend in Montana had the power and resources to protect her and Maya.

Chapter 2

Brandon Rayne lay with his face close to the dirt, wind whipping sand into his face like someone intent on sandblasting the skin from his body. Thankfully, he wore protective glasses that kept the sand from reaching his eyes. They also kept the heat and humidity contained inside the rubber seals. Sweat dripped from his forehead and down his nose.

He waited, his gaze intent on the scope, lined up with the door to a building believed to be the current location of a high-ranking Islamic State leader in Iraq.

"Holding steady, Boomer?" Irish said into his headset. Declan O'Shea, one of the more experienced members of his team, was positioned closer to the small mountain village north of Mosul.

"Holding," Boomer whispered.

"If the shit hits the fan, no worries, man," Fish said. "We've got your six. We're in position and ready to roll." Jack Fischer, the team lead for this mission, had the others ready to enter the village on command.

The main purpose of their current mission was to decapitate the head of the snake. In other words, to take out this particular leader of the Islamic State wreaking havoc on grounds once controlled by the American and Iraqi military.

With the sun setting behind him, shadows lengthened, making it more and more difficult to make out shapes and specific faces.

Taped to the inside of his gloved palm was the image of the man. His target. He couldn't miss. So many lives depended on his taking out this murdering Islamic State militant who'd orchestrated the sacking of many cities and towns, raped women, slaughtered children and destroyed centuries of historical structures and relics. He had to be stopped.

Black SUVs pulled up to the structure. Thankfully, at the angle from which Boomer was positioned, he still had a direct shot at anyone emerging from the entrance.

A moment later, the door opened. Two men in solid black uniforms, their heads and faces swathed in black, carrying semi-automatic rifles, stepped out. Behind them was a more portly man dressed in black, his face exposed, his long dark beard, thick mustache and even thicker dark brows making him easy to recognize.

Instead of the fitted black uniform, he wore the long white robe and turban of an imam. Abu Ahmed had a fierce reputation. Those who dared disagree with him were beheaded as a lesson to others.

Through the lens of his high-powered sniper rifle, Boomer locked in on his target and squeezed the trigger.

As the bullet released from Boomer's weapon, the man dressed as an imam looked up as if to stare into Boomer's scope. In that same moment, a woman carrying a baby stepped out from behind him.

A second later, a bright red dot appeared in Abu Ahmed's forehead, and he crumpled, falling at the feet of his guards. The baby in the woman's arms jerked and went limp.

The woman screamed and looked down at her baby,

her eyes wide and terrified.

The black-garbed guards crouched, bringing their guns to the ready.

Fish, Irish, Nacho, Gator and the rest of the team moved into action. From their positions closer to the structure, they picked off the guards. More militants poured from the building, overrunning the woman holding the limp child.

Boomer focused on the other militants, pushing to the back of his mind the woman, now crouched on the ground, rocking back and forth, her wails echoing off the hills, her baby pressed to her breast.

He locked on another militant, squeezed off a round and watched as the man in black fell to his knees then flat on his chest.

Soon, the SEAL team converged on the structure and entered.

Boomer's job was to cover their six in case more ISIS soldiers arrived.

Soon, the team emerged, carrying backpacks filled with documents and artifacts of their operation. Fish and Gator led a man at gunpoint. He wore the black uniform of the Islamic State militants, an angry glare pushing his thick black brows together.

Women emerged from the building, clutching the hands of small children.

One woman, who didn't have a child clutching her robes, pulled something small from beneath her abaya, grabbed the top of the item and jerked her hand.

It all happened too fast for Boomer to react.

The woman tossed the grenade into the group of SEALs.

Fish scooped up the grenade, cocked his arm and threw it as far as he could before dropping to the ground. The other SEALs followed suit and dropped where they stood.

The grenade exploded in mid-air, spewing shrapnel in a three-hundred-sixty-degree radius.

The women threw their hands up to cover their faces. But the damage was done. Anyone within twenty feet of the explosion took a hit of tiny, deadly fragments of sharp metal.

From where Boomer lay, all he could do was watch and pray his team hadn't suffered any deadly injuries.

Women and children dropped to the ground, blood running like little rivers from the many wounds inflicted.

The man the SEALs had escorted out of the building clutched his throat, sank to his knees and keeled over on top of Boomer's original target.

Women and children cried. Many lay unmoving.

Boomer whispered into his mic, "Fish, Gator, Irish?" He swallowed hard and held his breath. Someone say something.

"Fish here. I'm okay. Flesh wound to the right shoulder, and maybe my right thigh. Can't tell where all the blood's coming from."

"Irish here," Declan's voice came across the radio. "Took a hit to the calf. Flesh wound. I can walk out."

"Bit in the ass." Gator laughed, the sound strained. "Won't be sitting down on that cheek for a while."

One by one, the team reported in with their statuses and injuries. Gator called in support from the 160th Night Stalker Black Hawk helicopter team. Within minutes, three choppers landed near the small village.

Medics rushed to triage and help the injured SEALs, women and children.

From the top of the hill overlooking the small Iraqi village, Boomer continued to provide cover, the image of the woman holding her dead baby replaying in his mind, over and over. He'd been tasked to take out an Islamic State militant at all costs. The man had been responsible for the deaths of thousands of innocent people.

Boomer closed his eyes for a moment and pinched the bridge of his nose. Yes, there was bound to be collateral damage in just about any operation they conducted. But that didn't make him feel any better. The bullet, meant for Abu Ahmed, had taken out the ISIS leader and the baby behind him.

A baby's cry pierced Boomer's consciousness. He opened his eyes and stared up at a ceiling he didn't immediately recognize.

He cursed softly.

The cry sounded somewhere outside the walls of the room in which he lay in a soft, comfortable bed. Sunlight wedged through the window, nudging aside what remained of the night's darkness and the cobwebs of memories lingering in Boomer's mind. He wasn't in Iraq anymore, and the baby's death had been well over seven months ago.

A lot had happened since then.

A light knock sounded on the door.

"Boomer? Are you going to get your lazy ass out of bed?" Hank Patterson's deep voice sounded through the door's wood paneling.

"Tell me you've got work for me, and I'll think about it." Boomer scrubbed a hand over his face.

"Oh, I have work. Get dressed and come meet your new assignment."

Boomer pushed to a sitting position, the weight of his dreams still pressing hard against his chest. "I'm up." He swung his legs over the side of the bed and stood naked in the bright light of dawn. As the sun crept above the horizon, light filled the room through the window shades he'd left open the night before.

Boomer jammed his legs into a pair of jeans. He scrounged in his duffel bag for a T-shirt, sniffed, approved and pulled it on. When he stared at himself in the mirror, he shook his head. The T-shirt's logo read FUN IN THE SUN IN COZUMEL.

Boomer snorted. The last time he'd been truly happy had been his vacation in Cozumel. Before his last assignment. Before the death of that baby. Before he'd left the military.

One reason the vacation had been so special was the woman who'd set his world on fire. He'd spent the entire week with her, laughing, playing and making love into the wee hours of every morning. On her last night, she'd slipped out of his bungalow and out of his life, disappearing so completely, he'd often wondered if she'd only been a figment of his imagination.

Boomer had spent the next two days of his vacation desperately searching the island for her, but it was as if she'd never existed. The airport showed no woman with her name having booked a flight off the island. Her hotel room had been completely cleaned of all of her belongings, and no one could tell him where she'd gone.

He reached for the hem of the shirt, ripped it over his head and pulled on a solid black T-shirt with no logos and no associated memories. Montana and this gig with Hank Patterson and the Brotherhood Protectors was a new start at a life, post-military. Granted, he'd still be utilizing the skills he'd honed as a SEAL. Hank had insisted he wanted an expert sniper on the team he'd assembled.

Why Hank needed a sniper in the wilds of Montana's Crazy Mountains, Boomer didn't know. He still wasn't sure what his role and responsibilities would be. But considering Hank's was the only job offer since he'd left the military, he couldn't be too choosy. From what he'd been told so far, he'd be something like a bodyguard or a member of a special ops team, should the need arise to deploy more than one man at a time.

Other members of the Brotherhood Protectors team had filled him in on some of their assignments since coming on board as members of the Brotherhood Protectors, letting Boomer know the mountains of Montana weren't all that peaceful, and there were some crackpot zealots in the area from time to time. Terrorist activities weren't limited to the sands of the Middle East.

Boomer ran a hand through his hair, slipped his feet into socks and his worn black combat boots and left the sanctuary of the room Hank had let him camp out in since arriving two days ago.

Voices filtered down the hallway from the main living area with the killer view of the mountains. Two deep, male voices and two female voices from the sounds of it.

Then a baby's cry brought Boomer to a complete halt.

His heart raced, his hands clenched and he broke out in a cold sweat.

How, after all this time could he still be having these insane reactions to the sound of a baby's cry? Hank and his wife Sadie had a baby girl. He'd been around little Emma for two days, and he hadn't reacted like this when she'd cried. Perhaps the lingering effects of his dream had him jittery.

The baby cried again, the sound somehow different from what he'd grown used to coming from baby Emma.

Boomer drew in a deep breath, willing the tension away. He flexed his fingers, rolled his shoulders and stepped out of the hallway into the spacious living area, the Crazy Mountains the main artwork on display through the floor-to-ceiling windows. The sun had risen, bathing the room in a bright golden light.

After emerging from the darkness of the

hallway, Boomer blinked, giving his eyes time to adjust to the brighter lighting.

Hank and Sadie stood together. Hank had baby Emma in the curve of one arm. His other arm was wrapped around Sadie's waist. He smiled as Boomer entered the room. "Good. Good. Brandon Rayne, I'd like you to meet Chuck Johnson, Navy SEAL retired."

A big man with broad shoulders and salt-and-pepper gray hair stepped forward, his hand held out. The sun backlit him, making Boomer squint to see the man clearly. He gripped the guy's hand. "Always good to meet a fellow SEAL."

Chuck's grin accompanied his firm handshake. "Once a SEAL, always a SEAL?"

"Damn right." Boomer glanced toward Hank. "Are you telling me I have a partner for this assignment?"

Hank shrugged. "Actually, yes. However, Chuck isn't a member of the Brotherhood Protectors."

Boomer released Chuck's hand. "I don't understand."

"Chuck needs help protecting a woman."

Boomer returned his attention to Chuck. "What's the situation?"

"My charge has been relatively safe under witness protection for the past year. Until two days ago, when her cover was blown. We lost a man on the job and had to make a run through the mountains. I'm afraid she's in a whole lot more danger than I can handle alone. Since whoever has her number found her once, I'm betting he'll find her again. I need help when that happens."

"What did she witness?" Boomer asked.

"A murder."

"And the murderer?"

"Has gotten away with several killings. He's the son of a powerful politician with an expert cleanup team. Whenever the son commits a crime, his father cleans up the mess. His mop-up team is so thorough, they've left no evidence that can help us prosecute either the father or the son."

"This witness doesn't support a case?" Hank said, his jaw tightening.

"The body of the murdered woman never turned up. If my witness testified, it would be her against the son of a politically powerful man. They'd never get a conviction against the son. Which would also leave the father off the hook after all the laws he's broken protecting his scumbag son." Chuck shook his head. "She's a loose thread they can't afford to let live in case evidence of that murder ever does come to light."

Boomer frowned. "So what is your role in all this? Are you a U.S. Marshall?"

Chuck shook his head. "I was working with the DEA when I ran across the witness and got her out before she became another speck of dust swept under the cleanup crew's rug."

"DEA? Since when does DEA do witness protection duty?"

Chuck's lips twisted. "Well, that's where all of this is a little tricky. I wasn't really with the DEA. I was working on special assignment, following Harrison Cooper to get the goods that would nail the bastard and his father. When shit hit the fan in Cozumel where Cooper murdered a woman, I knew my witness had to get out alive. My assignment changed to protecting the witness."

"Who do you take orders from?" Boomer asked.

Chuck shook his head. "I can't say."

Hank's eyes narrowed. "If you told us, you'd have to kill us?"

"Something like that." Chuck raised his hands. "But don't worry. I'm one of the good guys. I'm still the same person who made it through SEAL training. I bleed red, white and blue."

Hank nodded. "I believe you. You had my back on more occasions than I can count when I was fresh out of BUD/S training and working my first few missions as a member of SEAL Team Six."

"Once a SEAL, always a SEAL," Chuck repeated. "That's why I came to you. I've been following what you've done with the Brotherhood Protectors. I knew that if we got into any trouble, you could help us out."

Hank shot a glance toward Boomer. "You're

in luck. Rayne just hired on with the Brotherhood. He's a highly skilled sniper, and has all the training you and I had. He'll be an asset to your cause."

"Good, because I'm not sure how long it'll take for the people who breached our safe house to catch up with us. I need to get my girl to another safe location where we can see what's coming and be ahead of the next attack."

Footsteps sounded from behind Chuck.

The older SEAL turned with a gentle smile and held out his arms.

A woman with long blond hair and green eyes stepped into the room, an infant in her arms. She handed the child to Chuck and lifted her head to study the others in the room, her gaze moving from Sadie and her baby to Hank, and finally to Boomer.

She stepped closer, out of the glow of early morning sunshine, and her image solidified.

Her gaze met his at the same moment. The woman's eyes widened, and her mouth dropped open in a rounded O.

Boomer's breath caught, lodged in his lungs, and his heart pounded a wild tattoo against his chest.

Holy hell! This woman couldn't be the one he'd met and fallen so hard for on vacation in Cozumel a year ago. The woman who'd disappeared out of his life forever. She had the same long blond hair and vivid green eyes. Surely, there couldn't be two women in the world who looked so much alike.

Boomer blinked, hoping to clear his vision of the mirage standing before him. Then she whispered, the sound carrying across the room, piercing his heart.

"You," she said, her voice barely a whisper.

Boomer's knees wobbled. He took a step forward. And another.

The baby in Chuck's arms squirmed, reached for the woman and cried out when she didn't immediately take her into her arms.

The tiny cry froze Boomer's feet to the floor, and his chest tightened until he felt as though he was having a heart attack. His fists clenched so hard, his fingernails dug into his palms.

Chuck handed the baby to the woman and stood beside her, facing Boomer. "This is Daphne Miller, aka the witness, and her baby daughter Maya." His gaze met Boomer's, and his eyes narrowed slightly. "This job would require protecting both Miss Miller and her baby."

"I know it's your first assignment," Hank said, "but it's an important one. You'd be more of a backup to Chuck in his effort to protect these two ladies."

Boomer heard Hank's words but couldn't move from where he stood. His gaze remained riveted on Daphne, the baby and Chuck, standing together like a family unit.

His heart sank to somewhere in the vicinity of his gut. A year ago, he and Daphne had made such a good connection, had spent every hour of every day they had in Cozumel together, getting to know each other and making love like there would never be another tomorrow.

Then she'd disappeared out of his life, only to turn up with this older SEAL and a baby.

A thousand questions crowded his head, but he couldn't voice one.

"Boomer, are you up for the challenge?" Hank asked. "I know you're new to the Brotherhood, but I don't have anyone else available at this time."

Boomer thought of all the reasons he couldn't do the job, but none of them left his lips. Perhaps what he'd felt in Cozumel with Daphne had been blown completely out of proportion. She might not have been as attracted to him as he had been to her. Obviously, she'd moved on with her life, found someone else to love and had a baby. By the way Chuck handled the tiny infant, it appeared the someone else was the retired Navy SEAL.

As the anxiety of the baby's cry dissipated from his consciousness, determination kept his fists tightened into knots. If Daphne could forget what they'd had so easily, so could he. Or at least he could give the appearance of having forgotten, even though a sharp pain seemed to have wedged itself into his chest near his heart.

Though he'd known every inch of her body, Boomer pretended like he'd never met Daphne, never made love to her, never thought he'd fallen for the pretty blond tourist on the small Mexican island.

"I can do this," he said aloud, fearing it was more to convince himself than to convince his new boss, Hank.

Hank clapped his hands together. "Good. Then all we need to do is position you somewhere private where you can see the enemy coming from all directions. Others from the Brotherhood can be backup in a matter of minutes, but for the most part, it'll be you and Chuck protecting Daphne and Maya. I'll have my computer guru work on tracking data about the politician and his son. Harrison Cooper, you said?"

Chuck nodded.

Hank shook his head. "Senator John Cooper's son. It's hard to believe the senator would go to such lengths to keep his son out of jail."

"Yeah," Chuck's lips thinned. "But again, we can't pin the cleanups to him. We haven't been able to capture one of the men. Whoever hired them got some pretty slick mercenaries to do their dirty work. They make it their business to disappear, only appearing when they have a job to do."

"And their current job seems to be to eliminate their one live witness," Boomer said, his gaze meeting Daphne's. She was the job. Nothing more. What they had in the past was just that—in the past.

She had a new life, a child and Chuck.
Where did that leave Boomer?
The awkward, odd man out.

Chapter 3

Daphne tried to breathe past the knot forming in her throat. She felt as if she'd been sucker punched. When she'd arrived in the wee morning hours at Hank Patterson's ranch, she'd hoped and prayed for help in her fight to stay alive.

She hadn't expected to run into the father of her child. Worse yet, he'd barely acknowledged her, as if he didn't recognize her. Or didn't care.

All these months, she'd fantasized about meeting Boomer again and telling him the happy news that he had a baby girl. She'd dreamed he'd be ecstatic and ready to take on the loving responsibility of raising a daughter.

But the stony, cold look on his face made her bite down hard on her tongue. Either he didn't recognize her, or he did and didn't want anyone else to know he and she had once been more than acquaintances.

Her heart skipped several beats and sank to her belly. For the past year, she'd dreamed of him, holding out his arms, taking her into his embrace and speaking of how much he'd missed her and how happy he was that he'd found her again.

Based on his response to her introduction, a real conversation would have to wait until they were alone.

"While you three decide what's next, Daphne and I will feed the babies." Hank's wife, Sadie McClain, with baby Emma on her hip, hooked Daphne's arm.

Though Daphne held Maya, she hadn't realized the baby was rooting around her blouse, searching for a breast to suckle. Her cheeks burning, Daphne ducked her head and followed Sadie out of the great room and into a small sitting room filled with morning sunlight.

Sadie settled into a wooden rocking chair, lifted her blouse and guided Emma to a nipple.

Unused to breastfeeding with another adult in the room, other than Chuck, Daphne fumbled with the buttons on her blouse and finally settled Maya on her left breast.

The baby latched on and pulled hard. The sudden tug made her milk come rushing in the expected letdown effect. Maya happily drank her fill while Daphne tried to think of what to say to the woman who'd opened her home to them in the middle of the night.

"I think breastfeeding is one of the most natural things in the world. I don't understand why people are so uptight about it." Sadie smiled across at Daphne.

Daphne stared down at her daughter, all her love bubbling up to the surface. Her joy temporarily crowded out the sense of rejection she'd experienced upon seeing Boomer for the first time since they'd created this beautiful baby girl. She swept aside the baby's soft black hair.

"I don't know what I would have done if I couldn't have breastfed her," Daphne said softly. "For the past year, we lived in the Utah foothills in a cabin with generator power. A refrigerator was a luxury that only worked some of the time."

Sadie shook her head. "You're lucky. Not all women are able to breastfeed. I like it because I don't have to carry around formula or extra water to mix with it. Whenever Emma's hungry, I can feed her." Sadie chuckled. "The only problem is I'm on call all the time. I have frozen breast milk for later use when I'm on the set and unable to be there for a quick feeding."

Daphne stared down at her daughter, still amazed at how much she'd gained in the past three months. From a tiny five-pound six-ounces to nearly twelve pounds, she'd taken well to nursing, keeping life on the lam less complicated than it could have been with a baby.

"I can't get over your wild ride through the mountains. Hank said you and Chuck rode four-wheelers into the mountains to escape the people after you. How did you do that carrying a baby?"

Daphne snorted. "Trust me, it wasn't easy. Chuck had purchased a special baby sling we kept with the four-wheelers specifically for such an occasion." Her lips twisted. "I never thought we'd actually have to use it, but it came in handy. It kept Maya close to my body when we got up in the mountains where it was much cooler, especially at night."

"The weatherman predicts our first snow will come sometime in the next few days."

Daphne shook her head. "After the heat of the Utah safe house, it's hard to believe it'll soon be cold enough to snow."

"We have had weird, unseasonably warm fall weather, but that's all about to change. Thankfully, you arrived when you did. I wouldn't be surprised to see a light dusting tonight. The temperature has dropped since you got here."

Daphne looked out at the beautiful mountains. "You have a lovely home." She wished to have a real home someday. A place she could raise Maya in safety.

"Thank you. It's fairly new. The original ranch house burned to the ground when I had a stalker causing problems."

"What?" Daphne stared at Sadie. "I can't imagine anyone wanting to hurt you."

"There are some crazy people in this world. Hank has done an excellent job hiring former military men to help protect those who need help protecting themselves." Sadie smiled. "You should be really happy with Boomer. Navy SEALs are highly skilled with every kind of weapon and hand to hand combat."

She dropped her gaze at the mention of Boomer's name, afraid her expression might give away the fact she was still in shock. "I hope it doesn't come down to a battle."

"Me, too." Sadie captured her gaze. "I could swear when you first saw Boomer, you recognized him. Do you two know each other?"

Daphne shrugged and shifted her gaze back to Maya. "He reminds me of someone I used to know."

"Boomer's fresh off active duty. He's been deployed several times to Iraq to fight against the Islamic State."

"Was he injured? Is that why he left active duty?" Daphne asked, trying not to sound too concerned or curious, but wanting to know as much as possible about the man she'd held tightly to in her dreams.

Sadie frowned. "He wasn't injured, but when his reenlistment came due, he decided he'd had enough. He hasn't said much while he's been here the past few days, but he has a faraway look in his eyes. Like he's seen too much."

Daphne frowned. "Are you sure he's stable?"

"Hank wouldn't assign anyone he didn't trust." Sadie glanced down at Emma. "Are you full?"

Emma stared up at her mother's face and grinned, with a milk bubble sliding across her lips.

Daphne realized Maya had fallen asleep while nursing. She pressed her finger next to the baby's mouth to disengage, laid her across her lap and buttoned her shirt.

When she was done, she tipped Maya up onto her shoulder and patted her back until the baby burped.

"Ready to rejoin the menfolk?" Sadie shifted her shirt, hiked Emma up onto her shoulder and stood. "I'd love to have you stay here with us, but I'm heading back to LA tomorrow. Maybe we can get our baby girls together for future play dates, if you remain in the area."

"I'd like that," Daphne said, wishing her life could be that simple. "I have no idea how much longer I'll be in hiding."

"Hopefully, not long. Something's got to give. You can't be expected to put your life on hold forever. Hank and his team will help." She led the way out of the sitting room and back into the great room where the men had taken seats in the bomber-jacket-brown leather couches.

As soon as the women appeared, the men all stood.

Daphne stared from Hank to Chuck, and finally let her gaze travel to Boomer.

Sadie stopped in front of Hank. "Have you all decided on the next move?"

Boomer stared at Daphne, his gaze less than happy, his brows pulling downward into a frown. So, he wasn't happy to see her. What did she expect?

"We're working on it," Hank said.

"In the meantime, how about some breakfast?" Sadie handed Hank their daughter and turned to Daphne. "Would you like to help?"

Daphne nodded. Glad to escape the room again. Maybe she was imagining it, but she felt a distinct tension stretching tightly between herself and Boomer. Staying in the same room without saying anything would be pure agony. She stared after Sadie, but Chuck stepped into her way.

"Want me to take Maya?" he asked, holding out his hands.

Daphne smiled gratefully. "Yes. Thank you."

"My pleasure." Chuck took the baby and cradled her in one arm.

Maya didn't wake; her mouth still made sucking motions.

Daphne hurried from the room, her heart full of her love for her baby girl and breaking at the lack of interest from the baby's father. She was so tired from their wild ride through the night and her heart was so heavy, she feared she'd break down and cry in front of Boomer.

That would be awful. No matter what his thoughts about the child they'd created together, she'd be damned if she let his indifference hurt her. She didn't need him to help her care for Maya. Lots of mothers raised children alone. Besides, she had Chuck.

At least until the troubles with Harrison Cooper were resolved.

Chuck had been there when the baby was born. He'd helped her through the first weeks of caring for a newborn infant, while recovering from the effects of having given birth. Chuck changed diapers and rocked Maya after the baby had proven to be colicky. The only thing he couldn't do was feed her.

If Daphne were smart, she'd have given up mooning over Boomer long ago and fallen in love with the man who'd kept her safe all this time. The man who'd been there for her and Maya from the start.

No matter how much she'd tried to imagine him assuming a more intimate role, she'd fallen short. She loved him like a big brother or a kind uncle. Never had she wanted to make love to him like she still wanted to make love to Boomer.

She stopped short of entering the kitchen, sucked in a deep breath and told herself to get a grip. Boomer wasn't interested in her. Why torture herself with memories of their last night together?

Boomer struggled to focus on what Hank was saying. His thoughts had followed Daphne into the kitchen. If anything, she was more beautiful now than when they'd met in Cozumel. Her breasts and hips were fuller, and when she smiled at her baby, the entire room seemed to light up.

Her baby.

Anger bubbled up inside. He glared across the room at Chuck. He had to be the baby's father. Though he had salt-and-pepper gray hair, those dark strands were the same shade as the baby's, lying in the curve of his arm.

How old was the baby, anyway?

Boomer studied the infant. She couldn't sit up on her own, so she had to be between two and six months, right? Hell, when did babies learn to sit up? He knew nothing about infants.

Chuck seemed to know his way around baby Maya. Had he moved right in and stolen Daphne's heart?

How quickly had she switched her affections from Boomer to the older SEAL? If he did the math, it hadn't taken long. Then again, if Chuck had been her handler since she'd witnessed the murder, falling for the big Navy SEAL could have been the natural thing. They'd been holed up together all that time, alone.

"Are you okay with the plan, Boomer?" Hank asked.

Boomer pulled his head out of the funk he'd fallen into and glanced across the room at his new boss. He scrambled for something to say that didn't make him sound like he hadn't been listening the entire time. "Could you go over it one more time? I want to make sure I have it right."

Hank grinned. "You and Chuck will take Daphne and the baby up to the mountain chalet near the Crazy Mountain Ski Resort. I recommend getting up there soon. The weatherman predicted snow as early as tonight. You don't want to get caught in the middle of a blizzard on your way out. Load up on provisions before you go, and stock up on weapons from the Brotherhood armory."

Chuck snorted. "You have an armory?"

Hank nodded. "When we rebuilt this house,

we had an armory installed in the basement. It's a vault with every type of weapon we might need to carry out our duties. As we've expanded our operations, we've added to our collection."

"Are they legal?" Boomer asked.

Hank smiled. "I wouldn't have it any other way. I wouldn't be much of a husband if I went to jail for something stupid. I have a wife and baby to consider."

Boomer's glance shifted in the direction Daphne had gone and then back to the baby in Chuck's arms.

"I knew we could count on you, Hank," Chuck said. "I've heard nothing but good things about the Brotherhood Protectors. Word of mouth gets around the SEAL network."

Hank nodded. "The brotherhood has made an impression, not only in the SEAL network, but throughout the United States. Some of our wealthier clients have shared their experiences with their friends. I can't keep up with the requests to provide protection."

"Are you sure you have the capacity to protect Miss Miller and Maya?" Chuck asked. "I don't know if my sources can afford to pay you."

Hank held up his hands. "I wouldn't take your money, even if you offered. Not all of our work is for pay. I have an ulterior motive here," he said, with a half-smile. "I'm hoping your experience with us will convince you to come to work for the brotherhood when you get tired of all the cloak and dagger B.S. with *whatever* organization you're working for now."

Boomer's fists clenched. He wasn't sure how he felt about Chuck. He knew for damned sure working with him on a daily basis, knowing he was with Daphne now, would rub him wrong on so many levels. He'd work this one assignment with the man, nail the bastard causing Daphne trouble and move on and away from the happy little family.

"Be careful what you wish for, Hank." Chuck shifted Maya into the crook of his other arm.

"If I didn't mean it, I wouldn't have said it." Hank nodded toward Boomer. "I'm bringing on new men every day. All of them have prior spec ops experience. They're ready to go to work the moment their boots hit the ground."

Chuck shifted his gaze toward Boomer, his eyes narrowing. "I hope you're ready. The people we're up against wouldn't hesitate to kill Miss Miller, her baby and or anyone who dares stand in their way." He paused. "We lost a good man in Utah. I don't plan on losing Miss Miller or Miss Maya." He stared down at the baby in his arms. "I won't lie. They've grown on me. I'd kill anyone who harmed a single hair on either one of their heads." His gaze locked with Boomer's.

Boomer agreed with everything Chuck said, but he didn't understand why he was staring across at Boomer as if warning him not to hurt the ladies. He raised his hand as if swearing an oath in court. "I'll do everything in my power to keep them safe." He turned to Hank. "You want to show us what we have to work with?"

Hank tipped his head. "Follow me."

Boomer stood and followed Hank out of the living area and down a hallway to a doorway with a fancy lock securing it.

Chuck, carrying baby Maya, brought up the rear.

Hank entered a code on the keypad and pressed his thumb to a fingerprint reader. The locking mechanism clicked, and Hank turned the knob, opening the door wide to allow the men to pass him and descend the staircase into the basement below.

Boomer reached the bottom of the staircase first. A motion sensor triggered the lights, illuminating the room in a bright LED glow. Racks of weapons lined the walls, and boxes of ammo were stacked on shelves.

"What could you use at the chalet?" Hank asked, passing Boomer to open a large cabinet. "Not only do we have weapons, we have surveillance equipment, GPS trackers, early warning devices and two-way radios in various shapes and sizes.

"I have my own rifle and handgun," Chuck responded. "We could use some of the electronics and radios."

Hank pulled out radios, small headsets and hand-held walkie-talkies, laying them out on a table. He dug in a large drawer and brought out a tracking device and GPS tracking chips. "I recommend you place one of these chips on whatever you want to track."

"Or whomever we want to track."

Hank nodded. "You can get lost really easily in the Crazy Mountains. But these are some of the best tracking devices that can be purchased. Be sure whoever has it won't leave it somewhere. They're only useful if they're worn or carried by whomever you want tracked."

Chuck and Boomer met gazes.

"Yes, we need to put one on Daphne," Boomer said.

"And the baby," Chuck added.

At least they were operating under the same assumptions.

No matter how jealous, disappointed or downright angry Boomer was over Daphne's decision to move on after she'd left him in Cozumel, he couldn't direct his anger toward the man who'd captured her heart. Chuck was a member of the Navy SEAL brotherhood. When shit got real, SEALs had your six.

Boomer selected a 9-milimeter handgun and looked around at the rifles.

"I've got what you need in here," Hank said.

He led the way to another cabinet, threw open the door, selected a rifle and handed it to Boomer. Hank crossed his arms over his chest. "It's a .300 Winchester—"

"Magnum with a Nightforce XS 32x56 scope and foldable stock." Boomer ran his hand over the stock and fit his finger through the trigger. "I had one in Iraq." It had been a part of his body—an extension of his arms and eyes. "It's a sweet machine with 100-700 meter accuracy."

Hank nodded. "More, if the operator knows what he's doing."

Boomer knew. He'd hit his mark on longer shots, including the one that had been taken out Abu Ahmed. The image of the baby behind Ahmed flashed in Boomer's mind. He closed his eyes to shut out the image, but the image had been indelibly seared into his memory.

For that split second, he had the urge to shove the rifle at Hank and escape the basement to the sunlight and fresh air outside Patterson's picture perfect ranch house.

Instead, he counted to five, inhaled deeply and opened his eyes. The sniper rifle was good for close range and long-range targets. He'd be a fool to reject it. Boomer tightened his grip on the weapon. "If it's all right with you, I'd like to carry this one."

Hank grinned. "I thought you would. I had you in mind when I purchased it."

Boomer's brows descended. "I've only been on your payroll for two days. You had to have ordered this rifle months ago. How did you know I'd come to work for you?"

With a shrug, Hank turned away. "I've been following you for a while."

"Really? How?" Boomer demanded.

Hank grinned. "Let's just say, I have

connections."

Which meant he also knew Boomer's skills had taken a nosedive the last few months of his deployment. Since the Abu Ahmed job, Boomer had found himself hesitating over every shot. He'd missed more than one opportunity due to his hesitation. Did Hank know all this?

Boomer eyed Hank, his eyes narrowing. While Chuck checked out the electronics, Boomer moved closer to Hank. "If you've been following me for so long, why did you hire me?"

Hank's gaze met his. "We all have our issues, but we also have the same, structured training. I wouldn't have hired you if I didn't think you could do the job. You're an excellent sniper. For this mission and others, I need a skilled sniper to take out the bad guys before they hurt others. Your reputation is stellar. I figured if you got off active duty, I'd be a fool if I didn't offer you a job in the Brotherhood Protectors."

For a long moment, Boomer held Hank's gaze. The older SEAL never flinched.

Well, hell. Boomer hefted the rifle in his hands. "I hope I don't disappoint you or your clients."

"All I ask is that you do your best." Hank's lips twisted. "That's all anyone can ask. And the best effort from a SEAL can be a whole lot more effective than that of a civilian."

"Damn right," Chuck agreed. "You got a bag we can put all this inside? I'd like to get up to the chalet as soon as possible and install some of this surveillance equipment."

Hank pulled a camouflage bag from a closet and set it on the table beside Chuck. "Take whatever you need, but please sign for the weapons. We have to keep strict accountability for them." He slipped a chart in front of Boomer and then held out his arms for Maya. "Let me have the baby, while you two get what you need."

Chuck handed over Maya.

The baby smiled and patted Hank's face.

Hank captured her little hand in his big one. "You are a charmer, aren't you?"

Boomer admired how smooth and easy Hank was with the baby, and wished he could be so open and relaxed with Maya. He heaved a sigh and signed the document in the space beside the .300 Winchester Magnum rifle and the handgun, and helped load the bag with the equipment Chuck had selected. He broke down the rifle into a couple pieces and stuffed it into the bag along with the rest of the equipment.

Once they had what they needed, Chuck handed the bag to Boomer and took Maya from Hank. He led the way out of the basement and up the stairs to the main level of the house.

"There you are." Sadie stood with Emma balanced on one hip. "Brunch is ready."

"We really need to be going." Chuck stared down at Maya. "Isn't that right, darlin'?"

"After you eat," Sadie insisted. "We have

sandwiches and homemade soup. And I've packed several grocery bags full of pantry staples, as well as an insulated bag of meat, cheese and other more perishable items. You'll need to use them up soon so that they don't go bad."

"I've got a couple five-gallon jugs of gasoline you need to take for the generator," Hank said.

"After you eat," Sadie reminded her husband.

The men filed into the dining area where the ladies had set out platters of sandwiches and a tureen of piping hot soup.

The men tucked into the victuals.

Boomer ate two sandwiches and a bowl of soup, focusing on his food, while trying not to let his attention turn to Daphne, sitting across the table from him.

Soon the platters were empty. Hank and Boomer helped Sadie clear the table and stack the dirty dishes into the dishwasher.

Daphne disappeared with baby Maya, muttering something about diapers and nursing.

Boomer took the opportunity to step outside with Chuck and Hank. The wind had picked up, coming from the north, chilling the air. Clouds collected around the mountain peaks, crowding out the bright morning sun.

The rumble of an engine made Boomer turn toward the long, paved drive leading up to the ranch house. A truck rumbled up the drive and pulled to a stop beside the house. A tall, blond man climbed down and rounded the hood.

Chuck tensed and reached for the handgun beneath his jacket.

Hank touched Chuck's shoulder. "That's Swede. He's one of the good guys."

Chuck dropped his hand to his side, but continued to study the newcomer until the big guy stepped up onto the porch and held out his hand to Hank. "I got here as quickly as I could. I need to get back tonight."

"Understood." Hank turned to Chuck and Boomer. "This is Axel Svenson, better known as Swede. Prior military, Navy SEAL. Swede, meet Chuck Johnson, Navy SEAL retired, current super-secret witness protection assignment. And Brandon Rayne, who recently left active duty. Navy SEAL."

Swede shook hands with Chuck. "East or West coast?"

Chuck grinned. "West coast."

"We won't hold that against you." Swede winked and held out his hand to Boomer. "I've heard about you."

Boomer's lips twisted. "I hope you don't believe everything you hear."

Swede snorted. "Only the good stuff. DEVGRU, right? The best of the best in Navy SEALs." He gripped Boomer's hand, practically crushing his fingers in a tight squeeze.

Boomer shook the man's hand, and then pulled his free, careful not to damage his trigger finger. "Yes, DEVGRU. Call me Boomer."

"Boomer." Swede turned to Hank. "What is it you need from me?"

Hank pointed toward the Crazy Mountains. "I need you to make a run up to the resort chalet to show these two where they'll be for the next week or so."

Swede frowned. "I was up there last month. There's no electricity unless you've had the power company turn it on."

Hank shook his head. "I'll get on that as soon as possible, but that could take a day or two. They need to get the client up there ASAP. She's got some heat following her. The sooner they get her there, the better off they'll be."

Swede stared at the mountains. "The chalet is perched in a readily defensible position. You can see people coming from a distance. Why are people after her?"

"She witnessed a murder." Hank dropped down the porch steps and hurried toward the barn. "I'll fill you in later. For now, we need to help them gear up to hunker down in the cabin, off the grid."

Swede's lips thinned. "You couldn't be farther off the grid in that place." He shrugged and followed Hank down the steps and toward the barn.

Boomer moved to follow as well. When Chuck didn't, he turned back, a frown pulling his brows together.

Chuck jerked his head toward Hank. "I'll stay here and make sure no one bothers the ladies."

Despite the gathering of clouds over the mountaintops, the morning sun still had a firm hold on the valley.

Boomer had a hard time reconciling the threat to Daphne and the beauty of the landscape surrounding him. But then, he'd been equally amazed by the glorious sunsets of Iraq and Afghanistan, where the dust lingering in the air turned the sky a bright, flaming orange.

Too often, US combatants were captivated by the beauty and forgot how deadly the country could be.

With Chuck guarding the house, Boomer followed Hank and Swede to the barn behind the house, where they proceeded to load a truck with every kind of supply they might need, including firewood.

The temperatures dropped steadily. The wind added a chill factor that made Boomer wish he had his winter coat. If he wasn't mistaken, he could smell the snow in the air.

"If we get the snow the weatherman is predicting, you might have difficulties getting down from the mountain in the truck," Hank was saying. He glanced at Swede and the two men nodded. "They should take the snowmobiles."

Boomer glanced at the brown mountains and the green grass in the valley. "Snowmobiles?"

Hank and Swede laughed. "You'd be

surprised how quickly snow can cover the ground," Swede said. "My first winter here, I got caught out in my shorts. Nearly froze my kneecaps off. Now, I carry a sleeping bag, a jacket and candles in whatever vehicle I'm in, winter or summer."

"I've seen it snow in July in the Crazy Mountains," Hank said. I went on a fishing trip with some of my high school buddies and got caught in a blizzard. Thankfully, we had tents and sleeping bags or we wouldn't have made it back down alive."

Boomer shrugged. "I'll take your word for it."

"It's better to have too many supplies than not enough," Hank said.

"True," Boomer agreed.

Swede slipped into the driver's seat of the pickup and started the engine. He pulled to the back of the barn.

"We can go through here." Hank led the way through the structure to the back where two snowmobiles were parked in a horse stall. He started the engine on one and drove it to the back door of the huge barn. He flung open the barn doors.

Swede backed the trailer up to the opening, shifted into park and climbed down.

"Know how to drive a snowmobile?" Hank asked Boomer.

Boomer nodded. "We trained in Alaska for two months during the dead of winter. I learned how to dress for the occasion and I have a healthy respect for the power of snowmobiles for getting around when there are no roads and nothing but snow and ice all around."

"Good." Hank nodded. "How are you on snow skis or a snow board?"

"I prefer skis," Boomer replied.

Hank turned to Swede. "Got that?"

Swede passed Boomer and Hank. "Yeah." He disappeared into what appeared to be a tack room and emerged with two sets of snow skis.

Boomer shook his head, staring out at the green grass in the pasture.

"Seriously, you can't base your predictions on what it looks like in the valley." Hank pounded Boomer on the back and climbed onto the snowmobile. "I've got this machine, you can get the other. After revving the engine a couple of times, he drove the tracked vehicle onto the trailer.

Boomer entered the stall, sat on the snowmobile and turned the key in the ignition. The engine roared to life and then settled into a steady hum. Moments later, he drove the vehicle up onto the trailer.

Like Hank said, it was better to over pack than go without.

Once they had all of the outdoor equipment stored and the skis tucked into the bed of the truck, Hank turned back to the house. "I'll go check on Chuck and Miss Miller. You'll take one of the company vehicles up into the mountains, while Swede drives the truck with the trailer."

Swede hefted a five-gallon jug of fuel from a row of jugs and set it in the truck bed.

Boomer loaded another, his gaze on Hank as he walked toward the house.

Before Hank reached the porch, Chuck stepped out, followed by Daphne carrying Maya. Daphne wore a ski jacket and held the baby in a sling beneath the jacket.

Chuck carried two large ski jackets. He tossed them into the backseat of a shiny black, four-wheel-drive, crew cab pickup. Then he held the door for Daphne and waited while she untangled herself from the sling and placed the baby in a car seat in back and buckled her in. Daphne slipped in next to the baby.

Chuck stared across the bed of the truck at Boomer.

"I'll drive," Boomer said, aiming his comment at Chuck, before turning his attention to Swede.

"Good," Swede said. "Stay close while following me up to the cabin. The roads can be tricky and the drop-offs are wicked." The big blond SEAL stared at the sky. "We better get going. I have no doubt we'll get up there in time to beat the storm, but I'd like to get back down before the rain or snow makes it impossible."

Chuck climbed into the front passenger seat.

Boomer slipped into the driver's seat.

Hank leaned into the driver's side window and glanced back at Daphne. "These two men will make sure you're okay."

Boomer glanced in the rearview mirror at Daphne. A tiny dent formed between her brows, and her eyes darkened to a deep forest green. Until that moment, he hadn't noticed the shadows beneath her eyes or the way she pulled her bottom lip between her teeth. The woman had worry written in every line of her face.

Her gaze met his for a moment and then returned to Hank. "Thank you, Mr. Patterson. Chuck's been great, but he can't be expected to do it alone."

"Hey, I got you out of the safe house alive," Chuck said from the front seat.

Daphne touched a hand to the older SEAL's shoulder and smiled gently. "You did get us out of the safe house. But you can't be awake twenty-four-seven. Even you have to sleep some of the time."

Chuck's jaw clenched. "I doubt Rodney knew what hit him. I sent Paul back to his family. We can't let Cooper's goons get that close ever again."

Boomer frowned. "What exactly happened at the safe house?"

"Our security was breached at the gate to the property. One of our guards was murdered in the process."

Daphne's gaze dropped and a tear rolled down her cheek. "Rodney was so young. He didn't deserve to die."

"Nor did the woman Cooper murdered,"

Chuck said.

"I'll send up reinforcements as my men free up," Hank said, clapping the bottom of the window frame. "I'd leave Swede with you, but he's on another assignment. I could only pull him for a day. I'd go with you, but I have a plane waiting at the airport to take me to Helena to meet with another client."

"We'll handle it," Chuck assured Hank.

Boomer frowned. He didn't like having another man answer for him. When they were settled in the cabin, he'd be sure to discuss ground rules and specific responsibilities.

And when he got Daphne alone, they'd discuss what had happened in Cozumel.

Chapter 4

The drive into the mountains did little to make Daphne feel any better about her entire situation.

How was isolating her and Maya in a mountain cabin supposed to make them safer?

So, they could see a vehicle coming before it reached them. They'd be stuck in the mountains, away from civilization. Just like before—and that hadn't been much of a solution. Granted, they'd had time to escape on the four-wheelers.

Daphne nodded toward the two snowmobiles loaded onto the trailer in front of them. "Why do we need snowmobiles? Don't we have to have snow in order to use them?"

Boomer shot her a glance. "Hank assured us the weather's going to get ugly. He predicts we'll have snow tonight."

"I would think, until the snow materializes, we'd have been better off with a couple of four-wheelers," she said, directing her comment to Chuck, the man who'd orchestrated their daring mountain escape out of Utah.

Chuck shrugged. "Hank knows Montana. If he says it'll snow, it probably will. If there's snow on the ground, I'd rather have snowmobiles up there than four-wheelers."

In the truck ahead, Swede took the turns

slowly enough not to lose their vehicles or put the trailer at risk of falling down the steepening slopes beside the narrow gravel road. By the time they reached the remote chalet, Daphne's hands ached from the white-knuckled grip she'd kept on the armrest.

She could imagine the toll the drive had taken on Boomer. He had a lot riding on him. Not only did he have a trailer load of snowmobiles to maneuver through the mountains, he had a mother and child in the back seat. Losing control was not an option.

The chalet, as Hank had called it, was a beautiful, woodsy structure that complemented the mountain terrain and would have been a peaceful retreat for anyone else.

Boomer turned the truck around and backed it up to the side of the shed. Once he switched off the truck engine, he released a long, slow breath and uncurled his fingers from around the steering wheel.

The baby squeaked from the back seat.

Daphne turned to her baby girl and smiled. She'd slept through the worst of the bumpy roads and harrowing turns. "Hey, sweetie," she cooed, unbuckling the restraints. She lifted Maya into her arms and caught Boomer staring at them in the reflection from the rearview mirror.

Was he as indifferent as he appeared?

Maya gurgled and cooed, grabbing a fistful of Daphne's hair. "Hey, baby girl," she said softly, prying the baby's fingers loose from the strand. "We're going to be okay up here." She spoke the words of assurance as much for herself as for the baby. Being in the crosshairs of a murderer had never been her idea of how her life would go.

Now, she had to shore up her courage and find a way to break it to Boomer that Maya was his baby. Thus far, he didn't seem to have a clue.

Chuck had been good enough to keep the information to himself. He knew exactly who Boomer was to Daphne and Maya, yet he'd held his counsel and refused to spill the beans until Daphne was good and ready.

Boomer slid out of the driver's seat and dropped to the ground.

Swede was already out of his truck, removing the tie-downs from the snowmobiles on the trailer. Once he had them loose, he climbed aboard one, started the engine and backed it down the ramp and into the shed.

Boomer followed suit with the other machine, climbing onboard and attempting to start the engine. He hit the ignition button and nothing happened. Again. Nothing happened.

"Let's just get it off the trailer," Chuck said. "I can look at it later and see if I can get it going. Might be as simple as a loose wire."

Between Chuck and Boomer, they put the vehicle in neutral and pushed it down the ramp, parking it beside the first snowmobile inside the shed. Both faced the door for quick and easy deployment. Assuming they both would start.

Daphne made a mental note of where the machines were. Chuck had skills with mechanics. He'd have the cantankerous one fixed in no time. And, after having to make a quick escape from the safe house in Utah, she knew the value of prepositioning. If they had to use the snowmobiles in a hurry, they could. Hopefully, it wouldn't come to that. Then again, their daring escape through the Wasatch Range had seemed like a farfetched plan, until they'd had to execute it.

As Daphne pushed open her door, a frigid gust of wind ruffled her hair, sending a chill rippling down the back of her neck. She stepped down from the truck, balancing Maya in her arms. She reached back into the cab, grabbed the blanket and wrapped it snugly around the baby.

Swede glanced up at the sky as the first snowflakes descended. "I'll take the trailer back down the mountain. But I need to get going." He tilted his head toward the northwest. "Those storm clouds are about to open up."

Daphne paused beside Swede. "Thank you for helping us."

He nodded and gave her half a smile. "My pleasure."

Daphne didn't stay out in the elements for long. She entered the chalet and closed the door, grateful the building blocked the wickedly cold wind. Though the interior of the structure wasn't much warmer than outside, just moving out of the wind helped.

She lifted the blanket and checked on Maya.

The baby looked up at her with big blue eyes and a smile on her soft pink lips.

Daphne's heart swelled with love for her child. "You're such a happy baby." She glanced around the room, locating a fireplace. The sooner they had a roaring fire burning in the grate, the sooner the room would warm. She hoped the men would unload the firewood first.

Daphne stood by the floor-to-ceiling windows and watched the three men working in the bitter cold. Once Swede left and they settled into the chalet, Daphne had to pull Boomer aside and break the news to him that Maya was his daughter.

Her chest tightened, and her palms grew clammy despite the chill air in the chalet.

Would he be shocked, happy or angry? No matter what, he had to know he was a father. For the past year, she'd wanted more than anything to contact him and let him know. Now that the time was near, Daphne's courage faltered and her heartbeat skittered inside her chest.

Boomer helped Chuck move the trailer to Swede's hitch. When they'd finished, Swede held out his hand. "As soon as I have a break in my current assignment, I'll head up here to help out. In the meantime, good luck."

"Thanks." Boomer shook hands with Swede.

Chuck emerged from carrying supplies into

the cabin and shook hands with the big blond SEAL. "Thanks for the help."

"Anytime." Swede frowned. "If I had more time, I'd set up the surveillance monitoring equipment."

"That'll have to wait until the electricity is turned on, anyway," Chuck pointed out.

"Hopefully, that will only be a day or two." A giant snowflake landed on Swede's cheek. "That's my cue. I'm out of here."

Boomer and Chuck stood side by side as Swede maneuvered the trailer around the cabin and down the narrow road.

Once Swede was out of sight, Boomer grabbed supplies from the truck bed and hurried inside. By the time he returned to the truck, the snow was coming down in earnest, the flakes big and thick. Visibility had gone from miles to a few short feet.

Wind whipped the flakes against his cheeks, the tiny ice crystals stinging.

"Put this on." Chuck shoved a ski jacket into Boomer's arms and shrugged into the other one.

By the time they'd finished unloading the food, baby apparatus, gas, weapons, generator, firewood and skis, the ground was covered in a dusting of white. The road coming up the side of the mountain was completely covered.

Boomer hoped Swede made it down the mountain before the storm worsened.

Inside the chalet, Boomer had to admit it was more than just a mountain hunting cabin.

Whoever had built it, had done so with a vacation destination in mind.

The structure was two stories, with a bedroom on each floor. The kitchen and living room were on the first floor with a walkout deck that overlooked the mountain and the valley below. Before the clouds and snow blanketed the sky, Boomer could see down the road into the valley below.

The chalet was in an easily defensible position, with clear fields of fire. With the .300 Winchester Magnum rifle, he could take out any threat before they could get anywhere close to the cabin and its occupants.

In the living area, Daphne had stoked the fireplace with the firewood they'd brought with them from Hank's. Using tinder and old newspapers, she was able to get a fire going, but the logs had yet to catch and fill the room with much-needed warmth.

She'd set up a portable playpen in the center of the room where Maya lay wrapped in thick blankets, only her face peeking out. Her bright eyes were open and curious. She squirmed, but couldn't work her way out of the blankets.

Boomer set a box of blankets and towels on the floor beside the playpen and stared down at the baby with the soft blue eyes and dark hair. She didn't look much like Daphne, but she was Daphne's baby, no doubt.

"She's a good baby. She sleeps through most nights now, and she only fusses when she's hungry or wet." Daphne stepped up beside Boomer.

He nodded. "She's beautiful," he said, and meant it. He straightened. "I'm going to see about setting up the generator."

"I'll help." Daphne offered.

"I'll keep an eye on Maya and see what I can scrounge up for dinner," Chuck said. "You two go ahead."

"I can manage on my own." Boomer left the room and stepped out onto the deck where they'd left the heavy generator. He checked the oil and gas levels then pulled the cord. The engine turned over, but didn't fully engage.

The door opened, and Daphne stepped out, wrapped in a black puffy ski jacket. She pulled the collar up around her neck and blew steam with every breath she took. "I can't get over how much the temperature has dropped. When we left Utah, we were still in the high nineties."

Boomer didn't respond, hoping he could get the generator going. With the loud noise of the engine, he wouldn't have to engage in small talk with Daphne. He pulled the cord. Again the engine turned over but didn't engage. It putted to a stop.

"Boomer," Daphne touched his shoulder. "We need to talk."

He shrugged off her hand and straightened. "We have nothing to talk about." He stared into her gaze, briefly, and then bent to grab the cord's pull handle.

He pulled so hard he broke the handle off the cord, and still the engine wouldn't start.

Daphne crossed her arms over her chest and raised her eyebrows. "I get the feeling you're angry with me."

"I'm not angry," he denied, though his response sounded terse, even to his own ears.

Her eyes narrowed. "What I don't understand is why you're mad at me."

He threw the handle on deck. "I know why you left Cozumel. I know you didn't have a choice. I know what happened. You don't have to give me the detailed explanation. I get it. Just don't expect me to be happy about it."

Her brows rose higher. "You know?"

"I know." He bent to retrieve the handle, tied it back to the cord and yanked with a little less force. The engine turned over, chugged a couple of times and then roared to life.

Over the roar of the motor, Boomer heard Daphne's words, "Then you don't want anything to do with your baby girl?"

Boomer's pulse raced, his stomach clenched and the snow swirling around his head made him strangely dizzy to the point he thought he was hearing things that couldn't be possible. "What did you say?"

She shook her head, her brows furrowing. "It's okay. I don't expect anything from you. What we had in Cozumel was a fling. Neither one of us had any expectations. We didn't discuss life after the island. We certainly didn't discuss children. Maya and I can make it on our own once this murder thing is cleared up." Daphne spun toward the door, her eyes glistening. "I've done my part. At least, now you know."

Boomer grabbed her arm and yanked her back around. "Woman, what are you talking about?" He bent and switched the generator off. The engine rumbled to a stop, leaving nothing but the wind howling through the trees for noise.

"You heard me," Daphne said. A tear rolled down her cheek. She reached up to swipe it away. "You had the right to know. Now that you do, I don't expect anything from you. Maya is my responsibility. She and I will be fine."

Boomer shook his head, his eyes narrowing. "Back it up about four paragraphs."

Her brows dipped. "Why?"

"I want to be sure I'm hearing this right. You said *your baby girl.*"

She nodded. "I did. Again, you don't have to do a thing. I'm perfectly capable of raising our daughter on my own. I don't need your help."

"Our daughter?" Boomer felt as if he'd been punched in the gut. "As in yours and mine." He touched a finger to her chest and then to his. "Not yours and Chuck's?"

She looked at him as if he'd grown a set of horns. "What are you talking about? Maya is your daughter, not Chuck's."

Boomer's head spun. Maya was his child? The baby in the chalet was his flesh and blood?

Daphne's brows dipped lower and then

raised into her hairline. "You thought Chuck and I...that Maya is Chuck's daughter?" She laughed, the sound strained and tight.

Boomer stood straight, unable to move, not a single word coming to his lips. The truth swirled around him like a tornado, sucking the air from his lungs.

"Do you think I would hop from your bed into Chuck's so quickly?" Daphne pushed away from him. "You bastard." She yanked her arm free of his grip and stepped back. "I thought we had something going on in Cozumel. That we had a special connection." She snorted. "I guess it was only on my side. I was just another girl in a sailor's port." Another tear slipped from the corner of her eye. She swiped it away and squared her shoulders. "Well, to hell with you. You had the right to know you have a child, but now that you do, you can stay the hell away from both of us. That suits you, doesn't it? Maya and I would hate to cramp your lifestyle." She marched toward the door.

Before she could reach for the handle, Boomer jerked her around and slammed her against his chest. "You were not just another woman in a port. When I woke up the next morning and you weren't there, I didn't know what to think. I looked for you, but you were gone, everything about you seemed to be wiped clean. I didn't know how to contact you, and the airport didn't have any evidence of your departure. You were gone, as if you never existed." That empty feeling of despair washed over Boomer like it had been yesterday when he'd woken up to find his bed empty, the woman he'd fallen for so completely missing.

"I had to disappear," Daphne whispered. "Otherwise, I would have been gone for real."

"I get that." Boomer brushed the next tear away with the pad of his thumb. "But you had a baby." He shook his head to clear the cobwebs and confusion. "Why didn't you let me know sooner? I could have been there for you."

She shook her head. "You were deployed. I had to stay in hiding. I couldn't contact you. They were watching, waiting for me to make a move. Hell, I didn't even have to make a move. They found us anyway."

Boomer shoved a hand through his hair as the enormity of her words sank in. "Maya isn't Chuck's baby."

Daphne snorted. "If you knew anything about me and if you'd have quit thinking the worst of me, you'd have known." She wrapped her arms around her middle, tucking her hands into the fabric of her jacket. "I love Chuck…like a father or big brother. In fact, I don't know what I would have done without him over the past year. But the father of Maya is the rat-bastard standing in front of me, thinking I could be fickle enough to hop from one bed to another." She turned to walk back into the house. "I don't need this aggravation. I have a life, and it began with Maya."

When Boomer tried to stop her by placing a hand on her arm, she glared down at his fingers curled into her jacket. "I need you to protect me and my daughter. Other than that, leave me alone."

Boomer's chest tightened and words rose up from his throat. Before he could utter them and put his other foot squarely in his mouth, he swallowed hard. The angry, determined look on Daphne's face stopped him cold.

The door opened from the inside, and Chuck poked out his head. "Daphne, Maya's hungry. I can change diapers and rock her, but I can't feed her." He stared from Daphne to Boomer and back. "I take it you told him?"

Daphne nodded. "I did." She pushed past Chuck and entered the chalet without another word to either man.

Chuck shrugged into his jacket and stepped out onto the porch. He nodded toward the generator. "Need help?"

Boomer nodded. Boy did he. The woman he'd fantasized over for the past year had figuratively slammed the door in his face. She wanted nothing to do with him. But she'd have to get over it. Baby Maya was his little girl. He bent over and braced his hands on his knees, his stomach swirling, his head spinning. "Holy hell, I'm a father."

Chuck placed a hand on his back. "Breathe, buddy," he said, his tone wry. "It's not that hard. At this age, all they do is eat, sleep and poop.

Save your panic attacks for when Maya starts dating."

Chapter 5

Daphne held onto her anger for the next hour, careful not to let Maya feel her wrath. She spoke to her child as she nursed, warmed by the glowing logs in the fireplace.

All the while, her thoughts churned in her head. No wonder Boomer had been so distant. He'd thought she had gone from one man to another without a break between. He really didn't know her. Or he held her to the same standard as himself or the other women he'd been with.

How many women had he slept with in the past year? Two, four, a dozen? Their week in Cozumel probably meant nothing to him.

He said he'd looked for you.

Yeah, but how hard?

Granted, Chuck had done a good job of getting her away from the little island off the coast of Mexico. When they'd arrived in the States, he'd arranged for fake identification. As far as Utah was concerned, Maya was Maya Jones, not Maya Miller or Maya Rayne as she should have been. And the Utah driver's license Chuck had given her had her name as Donna Jones.

As far as the US was concerned, Daphne Miller had disappeared. She hadn't filed a tax return in over a year, and she never had a baby.

She shifted Maya to the other breast, adjusted the baby blanket over her shoulder and Maya's head, and leaned back her head in the wooden rocking chair.

How much longer could it take to nail Harrison Cooper and his corrupt father? They had to make a huge mistake soon. One that would land them in jail and take the pressure off her and Maya. Once those two men were incarcerated, surely she and her daughter could settle into a nice little cottage overlooking the ocean and create a peaceful existence free of assassins and sexy SEAL bodyguards.

Maya fell asleep nursing on the second breast. By the time Daphne laid her in her playpen, the guys had the generator roaring outside.

Daphne carried bags full of groceries into the kitchen and unloaded them into the pantry. With the generator running, the refrigerator worked. She placed the cold items inside and hurriedly closed the door. Until the electric company switched on the electricity, they had to conserve energy. The couple five-gallon jugs full of fuel wouldn't last forever. Thankfully, they'd brought firewood, and she'd seen more stacked in the shed. At least they'd stay warm in the chalet.

Daphne found a pan in a cabinet, opened a large can of beans, flavored with tomato sauce and spices. She cooked the venison hamburger Sadie had packed with the refrigerated items and mixed it with the beans and tomatoes for chili.

Chuck entered the house, and with him, came a gust of frigid air.

"The temperature has dropped below freezing, and the storm doesn't appear to want to let up anytime soon. I'd say it's safe to say we're not going anywhere tonight."

Daphne smiled. "On the flip side of that, I hope that means we won't have to worry about Cooper's team descending on us during the middle of a blizzard."

"That would be my educated guess. You can't see much farther than the hand in front of your face out there." He shook the snow off his coat and hung it on a peg on the wall near the door.

Daphne leaned to the side, peering around Chuck.

Chuck's lips quirked upward on the corners. "If you're looking for Rayne, he went for a walk."

Daphne frowned. "In that storm where you can only see the hand in front of your face?" She stepped toward the door. "And you let him?"

Chuck caught her arm. "He only went as far as the shed. He'll be all right."

She bit her lip, wanting to go after Boomer.

"Give him time to digest the news. He looked pretty pale."

"Well, he'll just have to get over it. It's not like he has to do anything. I can take care of the baby. I don't need a man in my life."

Chuck's brows rose. "And what am I? Chopped liver?"

Daphne drew in a deep breath and relaxed the frown tugging at her forehead. "Sorry. You've been wonderful through everything. I don't know what I would have done without you through childbirth and the first three months of all-nighters." She hugged Chuck. "I know it was above and beyond the call of duty."

"Hey, you know I'd do anything for you and the kid. You two have grown on me. I like to think if I'd actually had a kid of my own, she would have been a lot like you. Flexible, good-natured and tough."

With a smile, she hugged him again. "You're not old enough to be my father. But you'd make a great big brother."

"It's a good thing we're not physically attracted to each other. Someone might get the wrong impression."

At that moment, the door to the chalet opened and a blast of cold air split Daphne and Chuck apart.

Boomer entered. When he spotted them in a hugging clinch, his brows drew together. "If I'm interrupting something, I can leave and come back later."

"Don't be silly. Supper's ready, and you look like you could stand to warm up a little." Daphne checked on Maya and returned to the kitchen to stir the pot of chili. She gathered bowls from the cupboard and spoons from a drawer and set them out on the small dining table near the fireplace. Among the supplies Sadie and Hank had provided was a box of saltine crackers. Daphne set a sleeve of the crackers on the table. When she started to lift the pot of chili, Boomer entered the kitchen.

"I'll get that." He carried the pot to the table where Daphne laid a hot pad on the wood, and Boomer positioned the pot on the pad.

Chuck held Daphne's chair for her. When she'd been seated, the men sat and filled their bowls full of the rich, steaming chili. Several minutes of silence passed while they ate.

The silence stretched.

Tension built until Daphne finally set down her spoon. Any conversation was better than none. She took a deep breath and threw out a conversation starter. "So, what's the plan?"

Chuck grinned. "My plan is to finish this chili. You make the best chili. But don't tell my grandmother, God rest her soul."

Boomer ate the last bite of his chili and nodded. "Thank you. The chili hit the spot." He took his bowl to the kitchen.

So much for conversation.

Daphne finished what was in her bowl and carried her dinnerware to the kitchen.

Boomer had filled the sink with soap and water and set a teakettle on the stove to heat water. "You cooked. I can pull KP."

"KP?" she asked.

"Kitchen patrol." He took her bowl. For a

brief second, their fingers collided.

A shock of electricity raced from that point of contact up Daphne's arm and into her chest. Warmth spread throughout her body at that simple touch. When she glanced up to see if it had the same affect on Boomer, she was gratified to see his eyes flare before he turned with her bowl to immerse it in the water.

"If you wash, I'll dry," she offered.

"No, you've done enough." Chuck entered the kitchen behind her. "You're not the chief cook and bottle washer."

"But you two are protecting us. I need to do something useful."

"Taking care of Maya is useful," Chuck said. "We can handle doing dishes."

Behind Boomer's back, Daphne glared at Chuck.

He tipped his head toward the living area. "I think Maya is stirring. I'd much rather dry dishes than change a diaper."

Foiled at her attempt to be close to Boomer, Daphne left the kitchen and lifted Maya out of the playpen. As suspected, her diaper was wet. Though the baby had been a trooper for their great escape, traveling via four-wheelers through the mountains without a complaint, she didn't like being wet, and she wasn't afraid to voice her opinion.

Moments later, Maya settled into Daphne's arms, content in her dry diaper.

The men finished up the dishes and put the

leftover food in the refrigerator.

The hum of the generator nearly drowned out the sound of the wind wailing through the trees and mountain passes. But there was no denying the storm had settled over the area and Daphne didn't think it would let up for a while. For now, at least, they'd be safe.

"Is there any hot water in the water heater, yet?" Daphne called out.

"We used hot water from the teakettle for the dishes," Chuck said. "You can see if the generator has been running long enough for a warm shower."

Daphne rose from the rocking chair and leaned over to lay Maya in the playpen. As soon as she attempted to let go, Maya fussed. "You poor thing. All this running around is making you nuts, isn't it?" She settled the baby on her shoulder and glanced around the room. She couldn't shower holding Maya.

Both men walked out of the kitchen.

Daphne grinned. "Who wants to hold Maya while I shower?"

Chuck held up his hands. "I want to work on that snowmobile before we lose what's left of the light outside." He slipped his arms into his ski jacket and hurried out the door.

Daphne faced Boomer for the first time since she'd told him Maya was his baby girl. She cocked her brows. "Well?"

Boomer's gaze darted around the room as if he was searching for an escape.

"She won't bite," Daphne said, with a slight narrowing of her eyes. "She hasn't even gotten her first tooth yet. She won't be hungry for another hour, and her diaper is clean and dry. All she wants is someone to hold her."

His gaze rose to meet Daphne's, and he sighed. "What do I do?"

Daphne hid a grin and settled Maya in Boomer's arms. "You can walk with her or sit in the rocking chair. If she gets fussy, sometimes lightly bouncing her seems to calm her."

"And if that doesn't work?"

"I'll be out shortly. I'm only a room away." She shook her head at the terrified look on his face. The man had to learn soon enough what it was like to care for his own child.

Daphne grabbed the bag of clothing Sadie had given her and hurried toward the master bedroom with the attached bathroom. Once inside, she leaned her ear against the door and listened for sounds of Maya's distress.

When she didn't hear any cries, she relaxed and smiled. Poor Boomer was way out of his element. Spending time with Maya would be good for him.

Perhaps it would make him realize how much he would want to be with her. And that, maybe, he'd want to be with Daphne again. And if wishes were horses…

She stripped out of the clothing she'd borrowed from Sadie Patterson when she'd first arrived at the White Oak Ranch, and pulled her hair up into a messy bun on top of her head. Then she stepped into the bathtub and pulled the shower curtain closed. When she turned on the water faucet, icy cold water poured out. She twisted the hot water knob wide open and waited, praying the generator had managed to turn the cold water warm. After a minute, she turned the cold water all the way off. At best the water was barely lukewarm. It would have to do.

She flipped the switch for the shower and gasped as chilly liquid ran over her shoulders. She quickly scrubbed her body. By the time she turned off the faucet, she shivered uncontrollably. The big, fluffy towel Sadie had sent along was heaven. She dried quickly and wrapped the terrycloth around her, tucking the corner in across her left breast.

Daphne recalled the large walk-in shower in Boomer's bungalow in Cozumel. They'd made love in that shower several times. She wouldn't be surprised if that was where they'd conceived Maya.

A sharp tug in the lower region of her belly reminded her of how perfectly they'd fit together and how attuned Boomer had been to her body and her desires.

She stripped out of the towel and stared down at her body. It wasn't the same as when she'd been on the Mexican island. Her hips and breasts where larger, and she had a little belly pooch she hadn't been able to work off after giving birth to her five-pound, six-ounce baby girl.

If Boomer saw her nude, would he still be attracted to her? Or would he be turned off by the changes in her body?

A baby's cry sounded through the door of the bedroom.

Daphne's breasts tightened, and she could feel the letdown effect of her milk rushing out to satisfy her baby's needs. If she didn't hurry and feed Maya, she'd drench herself with breast milk.

After tossing the towel over a rail, she hurried into a sweater and the thick, warm leggings Sadie had provided, forgoing the bra that would be more in the way than a help.

As she stepped out of the bedroom, she could see into the living room.

Boomer stood frozen to the floor, holding baby Maya out in front of him, staring into her screwed up face as she cried.

He didn't move, he didn't talk to her, he just stood like a statue.

Before Daphne could take a step, the front door opened, frigid air and snow blasting into the room.

"What are you doing?" Chuck's voice sounded from deep in the hood he'd pulled up over his head and ears.

Boomer didn't budge, didn't respond, just held out Maya, his eyes wide and his breathing coming in short, disturbed gasps.

Chuck reached Boomer before Daphne, took Maya from Boomer's hands and handed her to her mother.

Daphne hugged the baby to her chest and smoothed a hand over her head. "It's okay. You're all right," she said in a singsong voice.

Maya immediately calmed and started rooting around for her dinner. Daphne carried her into the bedroom and lifted her sweater.

Maya latched on and settled in for supper.

Normally content to let her daughter feed, Daphne found herself counting the minutes until Maya was full. Then she could lay her in her playpen and find out what the hell had happened to make Boomer act so strangely toward his daughter.

As soon as Chuck took Maya and handed her off to Daphne, Boomer bent double and rested his hands on his knees, dragging in deep ragged breaths.

After Daphne left the room, Chuck demanded in a barely controlled whisper, "What the hell happened?"

For a long moment, Boomer couldn't have answered if he tried. The image of the woman in the black robes, holding her dead baby to her chest, haunted him.

For the first five minutes Daphne was in the shower, Boomer had walked around the room, staring down at the beautiful baby girl in his arms.

Maya seemed content to snuggle close, pressing her face against his shirt.

He'd tucked her blanket around her to ward off a chill and paced back and forth across the room, praying the baby didn't wake before Daphne returned to relieve him.

Then something outside made a loud banging noise, like a limb hitting the metal roof.

Maya's eyes blinked open, and she stared up at him.

Boomer had never seen eyes so blue, or such a precious, beautiful face. And she smelled like baby powder and sweetness. He'd marveled at the tiny human who was his daughter. A part of him, sharing the same DNA. Already she looked more like him than Daphne. Would she have her mother's kind heart and good sense? Or would she be like he had been when he was young—wild, hard to control and headstrong?

His arms tightened around her. Or would the people after Daphne snuff out her little life before the baby had a chance to grow, play, learn and one day marry and have her own babies?

Maya must have sensed his distress. Her face screwed into a frown, and she opened her mouth and cried.

The sound had rooted Boomer's feet to the floor, sending him into what was like a video rerun of his last kill and the death of the Iraqi baby. The wails of its mother blended with Maya's cries, and Boomer's head spun between memories and reality. He didn't know how to make the woman stop wailing, and the baby in his arms wouldn't stop crying. He held her out at arm's length, but the memories wouldn't detach from what he was seeing in front of him.

Until the door opened, and Chuck entered.

Once the other man had taken Maya from his grip, Boomer felt as if someone had removed the bones from his body. He was hard pressed to remain standing.

"What the hell happened?" Chuck asked.

Boomer recognized it as the second time the man had asked him the question. He swallowed hard and closed his eyes to block out the image of the woman crying over her dead baby. "I don't know," he said. He couldn't tell the older SEAL he was seeing things.

Chuck shoved a chair behind Boomer's knees. "Sit. Pull yourself together and tell me what just happened. No bullshit."

Boomer sat for a long moment before he looked up into Chuck's face.

The SEAL didn't look at him with an accusing stare. A frown pulled at his brows, but it wasn't an angry one, but more of concern. "PTSD?" Chuck asked.

Boomer shoved a hand through his hair and glanced away. "Probably," he said.

"What are your triggers?"

When Boomer didn't respond, Chuck added, "I have flashbacks when I hear the sound of gunfire or the backfire of muffler. Fireworks set me off as well."

Boomer's gaze shot back to the big SEAL. "You have flashbacks?"

"A lot of guys I know have a hard time assimilating back into the real world." Chuck dropped another log onto fire, grabbed a wooden chair and straddled it backward. "We've seen too much, been shot at, and sometimes can't separate our pasts from our present. Some people take years before the sharp edges blur. Others never get over it."

Boomer snorted. "God, I hope that's not my case."

"What was your trigger?" Chuck persisted.

Boomer buried his face in his hands and whispered, "A baby's cry."

"A what?" Chuck leaned closer. "A baby's cry?" The older SEAL muttered a curse. "Wow. That's going to be tough to overcome."

Boomer nodded. "I'm a father, and I can't even take care of my own child."

"You just found out you're a father. You can't expect to fall right into being a good parent."

"I can't do it. That baby needs someone who isn't going to come apart at the seams every time he hears her cry. She needs someone who has his shit together. Someone like you."

Chuck snorted. "I didn't always have my shit together. Believe me. It took me two years after I left the SEALs to find my way. For one and half of those years, I sank so deeply into a bottle of booze, I didn't think I'd ever find my way back out."

Boomer stared across the floor at his

brother-in-arms, feeling more connected to the man than he had since they'd met.

Chuck had been through the same brutal training, conducted similar missions and probably had killed his share of civilians in the course of his duties. He understood.

"Don't beat yourself up over this incident. Work through it. I don't know what kind of coping techniques you can use, but do what it takes." Chuck tipped his head toward the bedroom. "That baby girl is worth it. She needs a father who can be there for her."

And Daphne needed a man who could take care of her and Maya.

Boomer shook his head. In his current state, he was more of a liability than an asset to them. They'd be better off without him.

Chuck leaned across and punched him in the arm. "Don't talk yourself out of being in that child's life. Or Daphne's, for that matter."

"If I can't keep it together when Maya cries, what good am I to them?"

Chuck pinned him with a direct stare. "How do you think we knew where to find you?"

"You came to Hank. I just happened to be there."

Chuck shook his head. "That woman in there had you on her mind from the moment we left Cozumel to the moment you appeared in Patterson's living room."

Boomer's eyes narrowed. "We only knew each other for a week."

"Some things don't take long to gel. She couldn't stop thinking about you. Through my SEAL contacts, I followed your career. I knew when you got out of the Navy. How do you think Hank Patterson found out about you?"

Boomer's frown dipped lower. "You got me the job?"

Chuck shrugged. "No, your reputation as a sniper and a kickass SEAL got you the job. I just put the bug in Hank's ear. He made the decision to hire you. Hank's a nice guy, but he wouldn't employ just anyone. You have to be right for his vision of the Brotherhood Protectors."

Boomer wasn't sure he liked the idea that Chuck had been the one to get him on with Hank's organization. Nor did he like the idea that Chuck had been spying on him for the past year.

What did make his insides warm and his heart beat a little faster was the fact Daphne had wanted to know about him—where he was, how he was doing, when he was deployed and when he came home.

The woman had been through a lot over the past year. Probably as much trauma as he'd suffered. Hell, she'd had a baby. That in itself was life threatening. And he hadn't been there for her.

The least he could do was make sure she wasn't harmed by the bastards trying to kill her. He'd sort out his own issues after he got her past the threat on her life.

Looking over Boomer's shoulder, Chuck

pushed to his feet. "How's Maya?"

Boomer turned toward Daphne. With her hair piled high in a messy bun on top of her head, a thick wool sweater and leggings hugging her long sexy legs, she couldn't have been more beautiful.

"Maya's asleep on the bed. We'll need to keep the fire going through the night to keep the house warm enough."

"I'll take the couch and feed the fire through the night," Boomer insisted. He couldn't screw that up.

Daphne nodded, her brows twisting. "Are you all right?"

Heat burned its way up his neck into his cheeks. He pressed his lips together in a tight line. "Yes."

"I'll take the bedroom upstairs," Chuck offered.

"Won't it be too cold up there?" Daphne asked.

"Heat rises," Chuck reassured her. "If Boomer stokes the fire all night, I'll stay plenty warm. Besides, I need to be up above the noise of the generator. I want to know when the storm clears. If it stops in the middle of the night, we need to be ready."

Daphne shivered. "Do you think anyone would be out on a night like this?"

Chuck shook his head. "No way. But if it clears off suddenly, the night skies can be as bright as day."

"Could they already know where we are?" Daphne wrapped her arms around her middle.

"They found us in Utah," Chuck said. "It might only be a matter of time.

Boomer glanced at the rifle he'd hung on the hooks over the door. "If they show up, we'll be ready."

"I hope so. I don't want the same thing to happen to either one of you that happened to Rodney."

"It won't," Boomer said. Not on his watch. He'd be damned if Cooper's henchmen got anywhere close to Daphne and Maya. They'd have to go through him to get to the two women in his life.

Chapter 6

Maya cried out, drawing Daphne's attention back to the bedroom.

She hurried in to check on the baby, torn between wanting to be with her daughter and wanting to know what the men were saying.

Daphne lifted Maya to her breast again, straining to hear the rumble of voices in the living room of the chalet. She wished she could be in both places at once. Perhaps Boomer was explaining his strange behavior toward Maya.

The baby settled against her and suckled, falling asleep every few minutes as she filled her belly.

Every time Daphne tried to break Maya's seal on her nipple, the baby woke up enough to drink more.

Finally, baby Maya fell into a deep sleep.

Again, Daphne laid her in the middle of the freshly made bed, swaddled in blankets and surrounded by pillows.

Anxious to get to the bottom of the trouble with Boomer, she left the bedroom and returned to the living room.

Chuck and Boomer sat close together, talking softly.

When Chuck noticed her, he addressed her.

They worked out the sleeping arrangements

and Chuck grabbed his duffel bag and headed up the stairs to the spare bedroom, leaving Daphne and Boomer alone.

Boomer poked at the fire, rearranging the logs to bun brighter and hotter.

He was avoiding her.

Which confused her. She was sure he'd swept her with a glance when she first entered the room. At that moment, she'd read longing in his gaze.

When he straightened and turned, he sighed. "Sorry about...before. Is Maya all right?"

Daphne nodded. "She's fine. With a full tummy, she'll sleep for the rest of the night." She took a step toward Boomer. "I'm more worried about you."

His lips thinned. "Don't worry about me. I'm here to protect you and Maya. I won't fail."

Daphne believed him, but she wanted to know more. "What happened earlier?"

He turned away. "I'd rather not talk about it."

She touched his shoulder. "Yeah, well, if it involves our daughter, we need open communication lines."

Boomer shrugged off her hand and moved away. "It won't happen again."

"How do you know?"

He glanced away, a frown denting his brow. "Because I won't hold her again."

Daphne flinched as if she'd been slapped across her face. Her heart dropped into her stomach, and she placed a protective hand over her belly. "You won't hold your own daughter?"

"I'll protect you two," he said, his voice rasping, "but I can't hold her. I'm not fit to care for her."

"What do you mean, you're not fit? All she needs is love. Isn't that all anyone needs?" Daphne stood before him, her eyes burning, her heart worn on her sleeve. This was the man she'd dreamed about for the past year. But somehow he'd changed.

He stared at the door to the cabin as if he wanted to make his escape. "Maybe I'm not capable of love," he whispered.

Though hurt by his rejection of her and the baby, Daphne recognized a man in pain. Not physical pain, but something that hurt him on a much deeper level. Pushing him to confess what had caused the injury wouldn't help. Not at that moment.

Daphne hoped one day he'd be able to tell her what had caused him so much pain he believed he wasn't fit to be her baby's father.

Although disappointed in the meantime, she'd give him the space he needed.

She crossed to stand in front of him. "Okay," she said softly. "We'll accept your protection. I won't make you hold Maya, and I won't ask anything of you that makes you uncomfortable. But I want you to know..." She reached up and cupped his hard jaw in the palm of her hand. "I'm glad you're here." She leaned up on her toes and pressed her lips to his.

When she dropped down and turned away, she was determined to run back to the bedroom before the tears started to fall. She hadn't gone two steps, when a hand grasped her arm.

The next thing she knew she was crushed to Boomer's broad chest, the air forced from her lungs by the iron band of his arms wrapped around her.

Boomer held her close, staring down into her gaze, his eyes dark with whatever emotion he was feeling. "You've haunted me since the day you left," he said.

"I never stopped thinking about you," she confessed.

He shook his head. "I can't do this." His hands tightened on her arms.

Daphne leaned into him, her unfettered breasts pressed against the hard planes of his chest. "Do what?"

"This." His mouth descended on hers, and he stole her very soul in that one kiss.

Daphne didn't care that she couldn't breathe, she felt as though she'd died and floated to Heaven. This was where she'd longed to be since she'd last been with him in Cozumel.

Boomer threaded his fingers into her hair, dislodging the messy bun.

The long strands fell down around her shoulders.

He fisted his hand in the tresses and tugged, tilting back her head to expose the length of her neck.

His mouth left hers and traveled down the sensitive skin of her throat to the pulse pounding at the base. His tongue tapped against it, and he sucked her skin gently before pushing aside the neck of her sweater.

Boomer nipped at her collarbone, tongued the flesh there and tried to push the sweater farther over her shoulder. When it wouldn't stretch more, he reached for the hem and dragged it up her torso.

The cool air hit her back, while heat from his body and the fireplace warmed her front. Her nipples pebbled, and desire coiled low in her belly.

Daphne tugged the shirt from his waistband, dragged it over his head and tossed it to the floor. She ran her hands over the solid muscles of his biceps and across the coarse hairs covering his broad chest.

Boomer kissed her forehead, captured her lips in a hard, brief kiss and then worked his way downward, bending to take one of her nipples between his teeth. He rolled the tip around then flicked it again and again.

Her body ached with the need to take what they were doing to the next level. She wanted to be naked, lying in his arms, filled with his lovemaking. Daphne slipped her hands into the waistband of his jeans and then lower to cup his firm buttocks. He was so damned sexy, her mouth watered, her blood raced through her veins and she couldn't get close enough.

A log shifted in the fireplace, shooting sparks and making the light flicker in the dark living area.

Boomer lifted his head. "We can't do this."

She shook her head. "Yes, we can." Daphne slid her hand around to the button on his jeans and pushed it through the hole. She stared up into his eyes as she eased the zipper downward. "You know you want to, and I want it as much as you."

"We're not alone in this house," he reminded her.

"We're alone in this room." She reached into the denim and circled his hard length, easing it free of the constraint.

Boomer tipped back his head and sucked air between his teeth. "You're making this hard."

She chuckled and ran her hand across his velvety cock. "That's obvious."

He caught her wrist and stopped what she was doing. "I can make no promises to you or Maya."

She froze, her heartbeat stuttering for a moment before it settled into a rapid tattoo. "I'm okay with that. We're here, in the moment. That's all I want." *For now.* She'd work on more, later.

Boomer cupped her cheeks and raised her face to his. "Sweetheart, you deserve so much better."

"I'll be the judge of that," she whispered and

leaned up on her toes, sealing his mouth with hers.

Boomer fell into her, his tongue slicing through her lips to capture hers in a dance of desire, thrusting, twisting and caressing until Daphne's knees wobbled, and she clung to him for support.

He bent, scooped her off her feet and laid her on the couch in front of the fire.

Daphne stretched her arms above her head, her body on fire, her core aching and empty, ready for Boomer to fill. The fire's warmth and the intimate glow it created set the mood.

Boomer kissed a path across her chin and down her throat to settle on one of her breasts. He teased, tongued and nipped at the areola until Daphne arched her back off the cushions and cupped the back of his neck, urging him to take more of her breast into his mouth.

He complied, sucking hard, flicking the tip several more times before moving to perform the same magic on the other.

Daphne moaned softly, ready for him to take it lower.

With excruciating slowness, he licked and kissed his way lower, tapping the tip of his tongue on every rib, dipping into her bellybutton and, finally, coming to a halt at the waistband of her leggings.

Daphne reached for the elastic band, desperate to shed the layers standing between her and Boomer.

He pushed her hand away and caught the fabric in his hand, along with the elastic of her panties, and pulled them down over her hips and lower, exposing the triangle of hair atop her sex.

A pulse thrummed inside her core, her channel slicked with her juices and she almost cried out for him to take her before she spontaneously combusted.

Boomer slid his fingers through the curls over her sex and dipped between the folds to tap that nubbin of sensitized flesh.

Daphne dug her heels into the cushions, lifting her hips. "Oh, please," she moaned.

"Please what?" he asked, pressing a kiss to the mound of hair.

"Please, don't stop," she begged, letting her knees fall to the sides, leaving her open to him.

"I couldn't if I wanted to," he said and parted her folds.

The first touch of his tongue sent her to the edge of reason. The second catapulted her into the stratosphere. She dug her fingers into his shoulders and held on as her body rocked with her orgasm.

He lapped, twisted and flicked that very special place until she could stand it no more. She had to have him inside her, filling that hot, wet, desperate void that had gone too long without him.

Daphne dug her nails into his skin and dragged him up her body.

He still wore his jeans, but she didn't care.

What mattered was getting him inside her so she could wrap herself around him.

He slipped between her legs, pressing his fingers to her entrance. One finger slid in. Her juices coated him as he swirled that digit and then pulled out. When he dipped in again, he did so with two, then three fingers, stretching her channel's opening.

"Please," she moaned. "I can't wait any longer." The tension had rebuilt, taking her to the edge yet again.

Boomer settled his big body between her legs. He leaned over, captured her lips with his and touched his cock to her entrance. When he pushed his tongue past her teeth, he thrust into her channel, claiming her in one powerful stroke.

Daphne raised her knees, cupped the back of her thighs and lifted her hips to meet him.

He pressed all the way into her, sliding easily into her dampness. For a long moment, he remained deep and still.

Then he eased out. His next thrust was hard and swift, followed by more. Soon he was pounding in and out, faster and faster.

Daphne dropped her heels to the cushions and pressed down, lifting her hips, meeting his every thrust.

Her core tightened. A tingling sensation rippled out from her center to the very tips of her fingers and toes.

For a year, she'd dreamed of this. That long year of not knowing what was going to happen to her life and that of her baby. This was where she'd longed to be, what she'd prayed for countless times.

Boomer thrust one last time and buried himself deeply inside her. He drew in a deep breath and then pulled out and rested his cock on her belly as he came.

He dropped down on the couch and pulled her into his arms, balancing precariously on the edge.

"Sadly, we can't stay this way." Daphne pressed her cheek to his chest, making no effort to move any further.

"I know." Boomer pressed a kiss to her forehead, squeezed her body against his and disengaged, rolling to his feet. He held out a hand and pulled her to her feet, gathered their clothing and led her into the bedroom and closed the door behind them.

Surrounded by pillows and tucked into her baby blankets, Maya slept peacefully.

Boomer dropped the clothing on the end of the bed and kept walking, leading Daphne to the adjoining bathroom.

"I have to warn you, the water is cold."

He chuckled. "We'll warm it up between the two of us."

Daphne purposely left the bathroom door open. "To listen for the baby," she explained.

He had lots to learn about babies and Maya's needs. But for now, she was asleep and her mother was hotter than ever and naked.

Boomer's groin tightened. The shower wasn't nearly as open and airy as the one they'd shared in his bungalow in Cozumel, but it didn't dampen his desire in the least.

Once the water temperature increased to just about lukewarm, he helped her over the edge of the tub.

She shivered, her nipples tightening into tight little beads.

"We'll make this quick." Boomer grabbed the bar of soap and worked up a lather.

She touched his arm. "Don't hurry on my account. My body will adjust to the temperature."

He spread the suds over her shoulders and across her chest, moving his hands in slow, rhythmic circles around the swells of her breasts, pausing to tweak her peaked nipples.

"Mmm," she moaned. "Already getting warmer."

He spent some time tweaking, swirling and squeezing each globe until she arched her back, thrusting herself into his open palms.

"You're making me crazy," she said, her voice low, gravelly and sexy as hell.

Boomer's cock sprang to attention. "We can't keep doing this without protection."

Daphne's lips tipped upward on the corners. "True. But then Maya is proof not all protection is one hundred percent fool-proof."

"We did use protection then, didn't we?"

She nodded. "Every time." Daphne grabbed

the soap, worked up a generous lather, started at his shoulders and worked her way downward until her fingers circled his cock. "But we don't have to go all the way to get satisfaction." With slow, steady strokes, she ran her hands the length of his staff all the way from the tip to the base. She rolled his balls in one palm and circled behind him with the other to cup his ass.

A groan rose up Boomer's throat, and he thrust into the circle of her hand. He wanted to take her, to bury himself inside her again, but he couldn't move out of the tightness of her grip.

Lukewarm water sluiced over his shoulder, washing away the suds.

Daphne looked up at him with a sexy smile and then dropped to her knees in front of him.

"You don't have to do this," he started.

"But I want to." Then she touched the tip of his cock with her tongue.

Boomer sank his hands into her damp hair and grabbed a handful, urging her closer.

Daphne opened her mouth and wrapped her lips around him, flicking the tip of his shaft with her tongue.

His cock jerked, and his fingers tightened in her hair.

Then she cupped his balls, pulling him toward her, taking more of him into her mouth.

He moved inside slowly, responding to the pressure of her fingers. Hell, he was on fire. Desire rushed like flames through tinder in his veins.

She clasped his buttocks and set the rhythm, moving him in and out until he was pumping like an engine's piston, in and out. Tension built rapidly, sending him up toward the edge. Before he spiraled over the precipice, he pulled free.

Her hand took the place of her lips, gliding over him until the rush of his seed had been spent.

Not until he regained his senses did he notice the water had chilled considerably. He rinsed the remaining soap from their bodies, turned off the water and wrapped Daphne in a dry towel.

With another towel, he squeezed the water from her hair then patted her face, neck and legs dry.

Daphne took over and dried his skin from the top of his head to the tips of his toes. When she was done, she handed him the towel.

Boomer wrapped the terry cloth around his waist, swept Daphne up into his arms and carried her into the bedroom. Beside the bed, he stood for a moment, staring down at their daughter, stirring in her blanket.

Maya whimpered and shoved a fist into her mouth.

"She's hungry," Daphne said. "If you'll put me down, I'll feed her."

Reluctantly, Boomer lowered Daphne to the ground. He wanted to lie in the bed with her and hold her close throughout the night.

With a towel wrapped around her middle,

Daphne sat on the edge of the bed and swung her legs onto the mattress.

Boomer lifted Maya and laid her in Daphne's arms.

Daphne let the corner of the towel drop to expose her right breast and positioned Maya's mouth over the nipple.

Maya nuzzled greedily, her head moving back and forth, her mouth open like a baby bird's. Finally, his daughter found the nipple, sucked it between her lips and pulled hard.

Daphne stroked Maya's dark hair and settled with her back against the headboard. "She has your hair."

"She does," he agreed. "But blue eyes?"

With a chuckle, Daphne glanced up at him. "Most babies have blue eyes for the first few months. I think they're turning green."

"Like her mother's." Boomer stood for a long moment, watching Daphne feed Maya, one of the most beautiful things he'd ever witnessed. His heart swelled behind his ribs with a feeling he had never experienced. Sure, he'd thought himself in love with Daphne back in Cozumel, but this feeling was a much stronger mixture of love, pride and wonder. They'd created a child. A combination of the two of them.

For a long moment, his chest tightened, and he couldn't move from where he stood.

"Do you want to lie down?" Daphne asked, scooting to the edge of the bed. She raised Maya from the right breast and switched her to the left.

Maya's little hand fisted as she suckled at Daphne's breast.

"No." Boomer grabbed his clothes and backed toward the door.

Daphne frowned. "Are you leaving?"

"I think it would better if I slept in the living room. For now." He turned to leave.

"Boomer?" Her voice stopped him, but he didn't turn back.

"Why did you freeze with Maya earlier?" she asked softly.

He didn't want to answer. But if he did, perhaps she'd better understand why he couldn't stay. Why he couldn't be a good father to Maya. "When I was on my last deployment as a sniper, my target was an ISIS militant." He drew in a deep breath and let it out. "He came out of the building dressed as an imam in white robes. The man was responsible for numerous murders, rapes and beheadings. I had him in my sights, and I pulled the trigger."

"Did you get him?" Daphne asked.

Boomer bowed his head. "I did."

"What happened?" Daphne's voice brought him back from his memories.

"At the same time I pulled the trigger, a woman stepped out of the building with a baby in her arms. The bullet travelled straight through the ISIS leader's head and hit the baby." He turned back to take in the sight of Daphne nursing their baby. "The baby died in that woman's arms." He didn't wait for her response.

He left the room, pulling the door closed behind him.

Yes, he was a coward. The sudden panic attack he'd experienced reminded him he wasn't fit to be a father. The image of Daphne cradling the baby was much like the Iraqi woman holding her dead baby. Chills rippled down Boomer's spine, along with an overwhelming feeling of hopelessness.

He was there to protect them.

What if he failed Daphne?

Holy hell. What if he failed Maya?

Chapter 7

Daphne woke the next morning to the wail of the wind blowing against the windows. Maya lay nestled against her side, having scooted closer to keep warm during the night.

A dull gray light filtered through the window. The morning sun was completely consumed by the cloak of the storm raging outside.

Maya stirred and whimpered.

Daphne changed the baby's diaper and then settled her against her breast.

Maya drank her fill and lay staring up at Daphne, blowing bubbles in the breast milk still on her lips.

"Hey, sweetheart," she cooed, smoothing her hand across Maya's dark, silky hair.

Maya looked so much like her father, it made Daphne's heart hurt.

Why, after making love to her twice, had he left the room to sleep in the living area? Was it the presence of the baby that made him run?

Daphne smiled down at her daughter. "You aren't so scary, are you?"

Maya's lips curled in an adorable smile.

"How could anyone not love you?" Daphne asked her daughter. She leaned the baby over her shoulder and patted her back until Maya burped.

The scent of bacon drifted beneath the door. Daphne's tummy rumbled. She wrapped Maya in her baby blankets and slipped out of the bed. When her bare feet hit the wooden floor, she winced at how cold it was. She'd have to leave the door open to the living room to keep it warm in the bedroom. Hopefully, the electricity would be turned on soon.

Daphne hurried to brush her hair and teeth. She dressed in the thick sweater and leggings form the day before. Then she gathered Maya in her arms and opened the bedroom door.

The air in the other part of the house was much warmer. The fire burned brightly in the fireplace, drawing Daphne to its heat.

"About time you two woke up," Chuck said from the kitchen. "Boomer and I have already eaten, but we saved you some bacon and scrambled eggs. I hope you're hungry."

"Starving." She settled Maya in the playpen near the fireplace but not so near that a spark could catch it on fire. Then she turned to survey the room.

A blanket lay neatly folded on the couch, but other than that, there was no sign of Boomer.

"If you're looking for Maya's daddy, he braved the blizzard to work on the snowmobile that was acting up yesterday."

Daphne frowned and cast a dubious glance toward the window. Snow scoured the glass like sand. "He went out in that? You can't see two feet in front of you."

"What can I say? The man was determined." Chuck scraped scrambled eggs from the fry pan onto a plate and added two thick slices of crispy bacon.

Suddenly less hungry, Daphne took the plate anyway. She had to eat to produce the milk Maya needed. Taking the plate to the table, she sat in one of the wooden chairs and stared down at the fluffy yellow eggs, her appetite gone.

Chuck grabbed a chair, turned it around and straddled it, sitting across from her. "Hey, why the glum look? Would you rather have had an omelet?"

"No. This looks great." She lifted the fork and jabbed at the eggs several times before laying the utensil on the table and pushing the plate away. "What's wrong with me, Chuck?"

He shook his head. "Nothing's wrong with you, Daph." He slid her plate toward her. "But if you don't eat, my girl Maya will go hungry."

Daphne sighed and lifted the fork again. "I wish I'd never witnessed that murder."

"For your sake, I wish you hadn't either. But then Cooper would be getting away with yet another murder."

"If his daddy's cleanup crew succeeds in finding me, it'll be a moot point."

Chuck's lips thinned. "Boomer and I won't let that happen."

She reached across the table and touched Chuck's hand. "I know you'll do your best." For a moment, she sat in silence, her hand still on

Chuck's. "If, for some reason, I don't make it, promise me you'll take care of Maya."

"You're going to make it, damn it." A fierce scowl marred Chuck's face. "And, by damn, you'll dance at Maya's wedding."

Daphne smiled and squeezed Chuck's hand. "That's the plan. But if something were to happen to me, I need to know someone will look after Maya."

Chuck stared at Daphne long and hard. "Don't you think Maya's father will want to have a say in who takes care of her?"

Daphne glanced toward the door, willing Boomer to come through. "Just promise me, please," she whispered.

Chuck touched her arm. "Maya has come to mean as much to me as you have."

Daphne turned and smiled at Chuck. "And you mean a lot to us. You're like the brother I never had and the doting uncle Maya needs."

With a sigh, Chuck took her hand, a brief flash of sadness making him appear older than his forty-seven years. "I only hope that one day I find a woman as smart and courageous as you."

A glance down at the way Chuck held her hand made Daphne's heart beat faster. Did Chuck have feelings stronger than that of a brother? She looked up into his eyes.

Chuck met her gaze, a crooked smile on his lips. "Boomer is a lucky man."

"Oh, Chuck. Please tell me you aren't..." she fumbled for the word, "you haven't..."

Daphne rose from her chair and flung her arms around his neck. "You know I love you, Chuck."

He pulled her into his lap and held her tightly.

At that moment, the door flung open, and a swirl of snow blew in on frigid air.

Boomer stepped through the entrance.

Daphne leaped off Chuck's lap and straightened her sweater.

Boomer pushed the goggles he wore over his eyes up onto his forehead. The frown he exposed shot straight through Daphne's heart. Boomer didn't say a word. He glared at Chuck and back at Daphne, drew in a deep breath and let it out. "Just came in for a wrench. I don't guess I'll find what I'm looking for in here." He pushed the goggles back down and walked back into the blizzard.

"I should go after him." Daphne started toward the door.

Chuck caught her arm. "Don't. Maybe if he thinks he has a little competition it'll help screw his head on straight."

Daphne hesitated. Boomer had the wrong idea, and she felt compelled to tell him so. "What if he leaves me to the competition?" she said, her voice low, almost a whisper.

"Then he didn't deserve you anyway. Any man worth his salt would fight for the woman he loves." He didn't say it, but the words *I would* were loud and clear.

Daphne was heartsick for Chuck who'd

taken good care of her and Maya, and who had been there when Maya had come into the world. She'd never suspected he might have more than brotherly feelings for her. The man had been nothing if not professional in his protection.

Perhaps the competition he'd mentioned had sparked in Chuck the need to fight for the woman he loved.

Maya let out a cry, as if she could sense her mother's confusion and sadness.

Daphne gathered the baby and took her back to the bedroom to nurse. Going to the bedroom was a way to escape this latest development between her and Chuck. But the quiet time while nursing Maya gave Daphne too much opportunity to ruminate about Boomer, and now Chuck.

Add a killer determined to take her out, and she had quite a mess on her hands.

Heat flooded Boomer's veins though the temperature outside had sunk well below freezing with a wind chill factor of twenty degrees lower.

He stood on the porch, letting the frigid air cool his anger. The snow-laden wind blasted against his cheeks. If he didn't get out of the direct force, frostbite would be the result.

He bent against the wind and trudged through the whiteout conditions to the shed where they'd stored the snowmobiles. At least inside the shed he wouldn't be plagued by the bite of the wind.

Once inside, he shoved the door closed and removed the goggles. With nothing but the wail of the wind pummeling the metal roof and thin wooden walls of the shed, Boomer was alone with his thoughts and, like the snow outside, they swirled around his head.

Seeing Daphne on Chuck's lap had sent a flash of rage ripping through Boomer's veins.

He closed his eyes in an attempt to unsee what he'd witnessed, to no avail.

Well hell, what did he expect? Daphne and Chuck had been together the entire year she and Boomer had been apart.

Chuck had been the one to protect her from attack. He'd been there when Maya was born. He took better care of Maya and Daphne, for that matter.

Of course Daphne would have feelings for the man.

Then why did she make love with Boomer the night before?

The rage surged again. If he counted the actual number of days he'd spent with Daphne compared to the number of days Chuck had spent with her, he didn't have a snowball's chance in hell.

If he counted the number of days Daphne had been on his mind throughout the year...

What did it matter? He'd frozen when he'd been left in charge of Maya. Though he'd made love with Daphne twice the night before, when it came right down to it, he'd run out on her and left her to sleep the night alone when clearly, she'd wanted him to stay.

Boomer had no right to be jealous. Chuck was the better man. He didn't have near the number of hang-ups Boomer had, and he obviously loved Daphne and Maya. He'd do anything to keep them safe.

But so would he. His chest tightening, Boomer realized he'd lay down his life for Daphne and Maya. No one would get past him and do them harm.

He picked up the tools he'd been using to repair the snowmobile's engine and went to work. If they had to make a quick escape, both machines needed to be up and running.

For the next hour, he tightened hoses and electrical connections and did everything he knew how to do. When he finally tried the ignition, the engine roared to life. He let it run for a few minutes to make sure it wasn't going to cut out again. Switching it off, he paused and tried the starter again.

The snowmobile sprang to life without hesitation.

Satisfied his work was complete, he shut down the engine and stored the tools in a compartment on the body of the machine.

When he straightened, he cocked his head to the side and listened.

Silence.

Boomer slung his rifle over his shoulder,

pushed open the door to the shed and stepped out.

The wind had completely died down, and the swirling snow had settled. An eerie quiet hovered over the mountain, now covered in a foot-deep, white blanket. Clouds clung to the peaks, the sun blocked by their thickness.

The quiet set Boomer's nerves on edge. He glanced toward the house. The generator had kicked off.

At that moment, the front door opened and Chuck stepped out, zipping his jacket. His gaze swept the hillside, the buried road and finally the shed where Boomer stood. He gave him a brief nod before crossing the deck to the generator.

Boomer closed the shed and trudged through the snow to the steps leading onto the porch.

Chuck was reaching for one of the five-gallon jugs of fuel.

"Out of gas?" Boomer asked.

"Yup." Chuck filled the generator's tank and set the jug back on the deck. "Although, I think we should conserve what gas we have. We don't know how long we'll be up here, or when we'll have the opportunity to get out for more supplies."

As much as Boomer wanted to hate Chuck, he couldn't. The man had been there for Daphne and Maya throughout the yearlong ordeal.

The faint sound of an engine drifted up the side of the hill to where Boomer stood. He frowned and tipped his ear toward the hum. "Are we expecting anyone?"

Chuck's eyes narrowed. "No." He hurried into the house.

Boomer took a position at the corner of the porch with the best view of the road they'd driven up the day before.

A moment later, Chuck came back out, carrying a rifle with a scope.

"I told Daphne to take Maya to the back bedroom and lie down on the floor with her."

"Thanks," Boomer said.

Chuck left the porch and walked through the snow to a stand of trees. There he knelt and raised his rifle, resting his elbow on his knee.

Boomer had a good angle and field of fire. When the vehicle appeared, he'd have the best chance of hitting the target.

Now, all they could do was wait for the vehicle to emerge from the trees.

Boomer breathed in and out, taking slow, steadying breaths as he stared through the scope, getting a magnified view of the road two hundred yards downrange.

A solid black truck emerged, moving slowly over the snow-covered road.

Boomer sighted in on the driver's side of the pickup, hoping to see a face. His finger caressed the trigger, without applying force. If the driver and the passengers of the truck decided to attack, Boomer would take out the driver first. The narrow road coming up to the house had a steep drop-off. One wrong move and the truck and its occupants would careen over the edge with nothing to stop them but the ground two-hundred-fifty-feet below.

Peering through the scope, Boomer counted off the seconds it would take for the truck to get close enough to the house to cause concern. In five seconds, the truck would be close enough the driver could ram the house.

Five...

The truck slowed to a crawl.

Four...

The driver brought the vehicle to a complete halt.

Three...

Boomer inhaled and held his breath, his focus on the driver's windshield.

Two...

His finger rested on the trigger.

One...

The driver's door opened, and a man stood up on the running board and yelled, "Boomer, Chuck. Don't shoot!"

Boomer pulled his finger away from the trigger and released the breath he'd been holding in a rush. Holy shit! He'd almost shot his new boss.

Hank Patterson waved from his perch on the running board, balancing himself between the body of the truck and the door. "Don't shoot!" he yelled again.

Boomer rose from his crouched position on

the porch, the rifle still in his arms, ready if for some reason Hank was being held hostage.

Chuck stepped away from the stand of trees and motioned for Hank to pull forward.

Boomer's eyes narrowed. From what he could see, Patterson was alone, but that was only based on what he could see. A full-grown man could be hunkered down in the seat, holding a gun on Hank.

The owner of the Brotherhood Protectors slipped back into his seat, closed the door and shifted his truck into drive. He eased his way up the narrow road, careful not to misjudge the edges and drop-offs.

When he finally brought the truck to a halt twenty yards from the house, Hank got out.

Chuck retained his hold on his rifle, as did Boomer, ready should a hidden threat emerge at the last second.

Hank lifted his hand as if in surrender. "You can put down your rifles. I'm alone."

Boomer nodded toward Chuck.

"If you don't mind, we'd like to make absolutely sure you aren't being held at gunpoint," Chuck said.

Hank's lips twisted. "I don't blame you. If Sadie and Emma were in danger, I'd do the same."

Hank stepped away from the truck and waited while Chuck examined the interior and the truck bed. When he was done, he lowered his weapon and announced, "All clear."

Boomer lowered his rifle and stepped off the porch. "We didn't expect anyone to come this way for a while."

"I wouldn't have come if I didn't have to." Hank tipped his head toward the door. "I'm here to add to the ranks of protectors."

Boomer frowned. "You have news." His words were a statement, not a question.

Hank's lips firmed into a straight line. "Where's Daphne?"

"She and Maya are in the back bedroom, staying low," Chuck replied.

"Good. I'd rather tell you two what we've learned before we break it to Daphne."

Boomer's gut knotted. Whatever Hank had to say wasn't going to be good.

The door opened, and Daphne stared out at Hank, her arms wrapped around her middle, her body trembling. "I heard you talking. Whatever you have to say, I want to hear."

Boomer moved to stand near her. "I don't like the fact you're standing outside. Anyone with a rifle and scope could pick you off."

"Nice thought." Daphne ducked back inside the shadows of the doorway. "Then let's bring it inside."

The men followed her into the house.

Boomer glanced around the living area noting the absence of the playpen. "Where's Maya?"

Daphne gave him a hint of a smile. "Asleep in the bedroom."

He nodded and turned to Hank as his new boss closed the door behind him.

Hank drew in a deep breath and concentrated his attention on Chuck. "Apparently, the bad guys got hold of your man Rodney's cell phone and traced his calls to you."

Chuck's jaw tightened. "I didn't call you on my cell phone."

"No, but you brought your cell phone with you, didn't you?"

Chuck nodded and pulled the device out of his pocket.

Hank's lips twisted. "This area is notorious for bad cell phone reception, but apparently, they managed to track your cell phone to my place."

Daphne stepped forward. "Sadie and Emma?"

"Are safely on their way to California. Sadie had a meeting scheduled with her agent." Hank inhaled and let out the breath slowly.

"How do you know all this?" Boomer asked. "Tracking a cell phone isn't something that sets off alarms. I mean Chuck didn't know he was being traced."

"No. But once they located my place, they hacked into our databases." Hank stood taller. "They're using some pretty sophisticated tools to get past our firewall. I have my computer guru working on shoring up our tech defenses. But in the meantime," he paused and glanced from Chuck to Daphne. "They know you're in the area. I figure it's only a matter of time before they find you."

Daphne's face paled, and she sank onto the couch. "What should we do?"

"I came up to provide support. I put a call out to others on the Brotherhood Protectors team. We should have three or four more men up here by morning. Your safe house here won't be safe for long. We need to bring you down from the mountain."

"Why not now?" Boomer asked.

"I want as many people between the bad guys and Daphne and Maya as possible, before we bring them down from the mountains," Hank said.

Boomer shifted his stance. "Wouldn't it be better to stay here and defend in place?"

Hank's eyes narrowed. "I thought about that. But I think it'd be better to bring them back to the ranch. It's not as remote."

"Then why didn't we stay there in the first place?" Boomer asked.

"I didn't think they'd find you so quickly. I thought this cabin in the mountains would be the perfect hideaway, until we could get more information on Cooper and his cohorts." Hank shook his head. "Now, I'm not so sure. They have a lot more assets to find missing persons than I'd suspected. For all I know, they could have followed me from the ranch here, despite my best efforts to keep that from happening.

Boomer shot a glance at Daphne.

Her gaze met his. "How soon can we get off

this mountain?"

"I want to wait until I have more of my men here before we try to bring you and Maya down," Hank said. "We're better off taking a stand here with as few protectors as we have, than inching our way down the mountain without adequate reinforcement."

"How is the road?" Chuck asked.

Hank shook his head. "Treacherous, at best. The snow hides the worst road conditions, including the places where the shoulders are soft and ready to crumble. The best bet would be to wait until the snow melts before attempting to descend with Daphne and the baby."

"In the meantime, I'd like to get out on the snowmobiles and see if we have any visitors to the surrounding area," Boomer said.

"That's a good idea," Hank agreed. "We could look for weaknesses in our defenses and locate high ground that could be used by a sniper."

Daphne crossed her arms over her chest. "For that matter, I'd like to see what's out there."

Before she finished speaking, Boomer was shaking his head. "You have to remain inside, in hiding. You're the only witness they haven't killed. That makes you a huge threat to Cooper. Getting out on a snowmobile would set you up as a target. And then who would take care of Maya?"

Chuck raised a finger. "I'll take care of Maya. We need to recon the area. If Daphne wants to get out with you, I see no problem. As long as she puts her hair up in a cap, and she wears a baggy snowsuit."

Daphne grinned. "Looks like I'm going for a ride on snowmobile."

Boomer swallowed a groan. "If you come with us, you have to follow our orders, no questions asked."

Daphne nodded. "Follow orders, check."

"You'll ride with me," Boomer said. He glared at Chuck. "I'll deal with you later."

Chuck raised his hands. "I don't know what you're talking about. I'm here to protect Maya. What you and Daphne do is up to you. Just keep the noise down in the middle of the night."

Boomer's brow lowered. He hooked Daphne's arm and marched her to the door, and shoved her jacket into her arms.

"*Now* you're eager to get me outside," she grumbled. "Damn right I'm going."

"Damn right, you are."

She pushed her arms into the jacket and shrugged it over her shoulders. She arched an eyebrow. "Aren't you afraid I'll be shot at?"

"I might strangle you before someone has the chance," he said, opening the door and waving her through it.

"Some bodyguard," she muttered and stepped out onto the porch.

"Stay in the shadows," Boomer commanded.

"Staying," she shot back.

Once he closed the chalet door, he gripped her arm and spun her to face him. "What the hell are you trying to prove?"

"I'm not trying to prove anything." She lifted her chin and braced her feet slightly apart, as if she were preparing for a fight.

"If Cooper's cleanup team is out here, you're barely safe inside the house. Outside, you're a damned target."

She spun away from him and paced a few steps across the deck. "I'm tired of playing it safe. I've been holed up for a year." She turned to face him. "*A year.*" Her lips thinned into a straight line. "Maybe it's time to lure these bastards out of hiding so we know what we're dealing with."

"And if something happens to you, what will become of the baby?"

Chapter 8

Daphne's eyes narrowed. "If something happens to me, Maya's father will have to raise her." A frown tugged her brow downward, and a sick feeling settled in her belly. "Is that what you're afraid of? Afraid you'll be stuck with a baby to raise? A little girl who'll need you to brush her hair and get her ready for school every day? Someone who will be forced to rely on you to provide for, care for and love her for as long as you live?"

Boomer didn't move. He stared at her, a muscle twitching in his jaw.

"That's it, isn't it?" Daphne snorted. "You're the highly trained SEAL with the ability to gun down a man at four hundred meters without blinking an eye. You can kill a man with your bare hands, and you can race into an enemy-infested building without fear." She shook her head. "But when it comes to that little baby in there—your little girl—you can't handle the thought of being responsible for her life."

"You don't understand," he said, his voice choked, and turned away.

"Maybe I don't, but you're not doing anything to help clarify." She touched his arm. "Tell me."

He spun and gripped her arm so hard, it

hurt. "I've seen things." His Adam's apple rose and fell as he swallowed hard. "I've done things I'm not proud of. Things I can't undo or take back."

The anguish in Boomer's eyes cut through Daphne's heart. "That's the past." She pointed toward the house. "You have a possible future in there. One where you're a part of your daughter's life." Daphne held up her hands. "But if you can't or don't want to be included in her upbringing, I can't force you, nor will I try." She dropped her arms to her sides, her chest aching with longing for this man to take part in his daughter's life. "I don't expect you to be a part of my life if you can't find it in your heart to love me. But Maya is your daughter. A piece of you lives inside of her. For so long, I hoped you could love her, and that she would know her father."

Daphne drew in a deep breath and turned to look over the mountains. She should be filled with joy at the beauty of her surroundings, but her heart hurt too much for her to see it.

"Daphne, I need time," Boomer said. He touched her arm.

She flinched.

His hand fell away from her. "I don't know if I'll be a fit parent to Maya." He paused. "Chuck loves you and Maya. He'd make a much better father for her."

Daphne spun, anger replacing sadness. "But he's not her father." She poked her finger into his chest. "You are."

Boomer grabbed her finger and held it, his eyes widening, his gaze shooting past her. "Shh."

"I will not be shushed," Daphne said, her voice rising. "That little girl needs a father. She needs you."

Boomer touched a finger to her lips and then spun her around, pushing her behind him. "Be quiet." He leaned on the porch railing and stared up at the sky.

For a moment, Daphne's anger burned until she realized Boomer was staring up at the sky, his head tilted as if he were listening to something.

Then Daphne picked up on the soft humming sound. Her anger disappeared, and she leaned toward Boomer. "What is it?"

"An engine. It's too quiet to be an airplane or helicopter. But it sounds like it's in the sky."

"Are you sure it's not echoing off the hillsides? Could it be a vehicle coming up the road?"

Boomer shook his head. "I've heard this sound before. "Get back in the shadows," he commanded. "Damn. There it is." He pointed toward the cloud-laden sky.

Daphne stared hard but couldn't see what he was seeing.

"I don't see anything."

"It's a drone." He backed away from the railing, flung open the front door and ushered Daphne into the chalet.

Hank and Chuck looked up from where they

sat at the table. "Did you two get everything ironed out between you," Chuck asked.

Boomer shook his head. "I think they've found us."

Daphne's heart slipped into her belly. Her gaze went to Maya in Chuck's arms. "I thought we'd have more time."

"Apparently not," Boomer said. "There's a drone hovering nearby."

Hank pushed to his feet and strode toward the door. "Could you tell if it was equipped with anything more than a camera?"

"It appeared to be something that could be purchased by anyone. Not like the weaponized UAVs we flew over Iraq and Afghanistan." Boomer held the door for his boss, balancing the sniper rifle in his other hand. He glanced at Daphne. "Will you please stay inside for now?"

She nodded.

Hank and Boomer stepped out on the porch, closing the door to keep the warm air in and the cool air out.

Daphne paced the living room floor. "I can't keep dragging Maya all over the countryside. The weather's too cold, and the roads are too dangerous.

"Then we'll have to come up with another plan," Chuck said. He cradled Maya in one of his big arms.

"They want me, and they're ruthless enough to kill anyone in the way." Her heart flipped over. "I need to get Maya away from me. I could never live with myself if she becomes collateral damage." Daphne choked on the last word and stared at Chuck through blurred eyes. A single tear slipped down her cheek. "If I have to send her away from me, so be it. Until we stop these attacks, I need to take the danger away from her."

Chuck nodded. "You have a good point."

A loud bang sounded from the porch.

Daphne jumped. "What the hell?"

Chuck dropped to his knees on the floor, clutching Maya to his chest.

Boomer and Hank entered the chalet, their faces set in tight lines.

"What was the gunfire all about?" Chuck asked.

"I shot at the drone, but it was already dropping below the horizon," Boomer said. "It got away."

"It doesn't matter," Hank said. "The damage is already done. They know we're here."

Daphne held out her hands toward Chuck.

The older SEAL handed Maya over to her.

She held her baby against her breast, her heart racing, the fear threatening to overwhelm her. "What's to keep them from targeting this entire chalet? They killed a guard last time and blew up the safe house. We were lucky to get out in time."

"We don't know how they will attack next," Hank said.

"Exactly. And we can't keep running. Maya

made one mountain escape, but she's a baby. We can't keep jerking her around."

Hank nodded. "My men should be here by morning."

"That might be too late," Boomer pointed out, his gaze on the baby in Daphne's arms.

"We need to get Cooper's killers away from this cabin. Away from Maya," Daphne said. "The only way to do that is to get me away from Maya." She stared down at her child. Maya had only been with her for three months, but she couldn't conceive of life without her. She loved her little girl more than she ever could have imagined.

"What can we do to draw them away from Maya?" Hank asked.

"Use me as bait," Daphne answered without hesitation. "We have the two snowmobiles. If I'm on the back of one of them, I can leave my hair free. It'll let them know for certain it's me."

Boomer was already shaking his head. "If you're on the back, you aren't protected."

She looked from Boomer to Chuck to Hank. "Then give me a bullet-proof vest. The hair has to be out, or they won't fall for it."

Boomer gripped her arms. "I was okay with you being on the snowmobile when you would be bundled up like one of the men. But you're painting a target on your back for them to aim at."

She stared up into his face, her jaw tightening. "I'd die rather than put my daughter at risk of being caught in the middle. She deserves to live a full and happy life."

"Yes, she does. But we can get her down the mountain and to safety without you sacrificing yourself." Boomer smoothed a hand along her cheek. "Your life is just as important."

"What if they bring in men on a helicopter?" Daphne asked.

Boomer snorted. "Then we're all in trouble."

"Exactly." Daphne gripped his hands. "And all the more reason for me to get as far away from Maya as possible, draw them away, until we know she's in a safe place."

"The possibility of Cooper's men getting their hands on a helicopter gunship is slim to none," Boomer said.

"But he had a drone," Hank said. "They know where we are. Maybe they won't have a helicopter, but who says they won't have some kind of rocket-propelled grenade? They could lob a rocket into the chalet and kill us all."

Chuck shook his head. "You're getting ahead of the situation."

"Well, it beats being in reaction mode." She stared around the room at the three men. "I know it might seem farfetched, but these men mean business. They've proven effective at squelching others. I have to take them away from Maya. If we can distract them long enough, Chuck could drive Maya to Hank's ranch where the other Brotherhood Protectors could provide support."

"That leaves Maya with only one protector," Hank reminded her.

Daphne patted her chest. "But it's me they're after."

Boomer and Hank exchanged glances.

"We could wait it out here until morning. We don't even know if Cooper's cleanup crew is close. The drone could have been a probe. They might not be close enough to cause trouble yet."

Daphne held Maya closer. "Or they might be over the next hill, ready to hit this place hard with whatever they have. At the very least, they could have automatic rifles or machine guns that could cut this building into pieces, like we see in the documentaries on the wars in the Middle East. I'm not willing to sit around and wait to find out."

Hank walked to the window. "Daphne has a point. But if we do this and use her as bait, we have to be sure they know she's on the snowmobile, or they'll attack the house anyway."

"So we wait and watch for them to arrive," Daphne leaned forward. "But we have to be ready to go and keep them on our trail, but far enough ahead, so they won't be able to shoot us."

"I don't like it," Boomer said. "Just because you wear a vest doesn't protect all of you. If these guys are worth their salt, they could go for the head."

"She can wear a helmet," Hank said.

Boomer glared at his boss. "I thought we

were here to protect her, not put her out there for the crazies to take pot shots at."

Daphne planted a fist on her hip. "Would you rather they shoot at me, or blow up this house with Maya in it?"

Boomer frowned. "I'd rather not have either scenario happen."

"And I'd do anything to protect my child." Daphne threw the words at him, knowing it was a challenge. She wanted him to care about Maya.

Maya, sensing her mother's distress, whimpered.

Instead of holding her close, Daphne held the baby out to Boomer. "You choose who will die. Me or Maya, or both."

Boomer took the child shoved into his hands and held her out in front of him.

Maya squirmed and then stared at Boomer, her eyes wide. At first she appeared frightened and ready to let out a wail, but she continued to stare until a smile curled the corners of her lips, and she batted at Boomer with a chubby fist.

Daphne's heart squeezed hard in her chest. She willed the man to hold the baby close and love her like a regular father. After a couple minutes, she'd almost given up hope, when he pulled the baby in, wrapped his arms around her and smiled down at Maya.

Boomer couldn't get over how much Maya looked like him. It thrilled and scared him all in the same breath.

Maya swung her arm and caught him on his chin.

Boomer grabbed her fist with his free hand and laid it against his cheek.

Maya giggled and bunched her fingers, then tried to grab a handful of Boomer's face.

His lips twitched as if he fought a smile. "Are all babies this soft?" he asked in wonder.

Daphne's eyes glazed, and she nodded.

"Don't let that soft skin and sweet baby scent deceive you," Chuck said with a smile. "Maya's got quite a swing." He rubbed the corner of his eye. "She almost gave me a black eye the other day. She'll give the boys a run for their money when she's old enough to date."

Boomer frowned.

Daphne touched his arm. "Please. I want her to live to date. Even if it's hard to let her out of the house with a teenage boy. She deserves a life."

Boomer looked across the baby's soft dark hair to her mother and then to Chuck. "Do you think you could get her down the mountain without any trouble?"

Chuck nodded. "If you keep the cleanup team busy, I'll get her down and take her to Hank's ranch."

"The arms room is a reinforced bunker," Hank said. "If you can get Maya there, you two will be all right until the other Brotherhood Protectors arrive." Hank gave him the access code and the workaround for the fingerprint.

Chuck glanced toward the window. "Days are getting shorter. We have what's left of the afternoon to make this happen. And that's assuming the cleanup team isn't right behind the drone."

"We should get the snowmobiles ready," Hank said. "We can pull them up to the house so we can make our move if we hear anything."

"Or we can go out and see what we can find," Daphne suggested.

Boomer arched a brow, impressed with her courage, even as her confidence rankled. He wanted her safe, not daring some spec ops bastard to take a bead on her. "We don't want to stumble on the attack team."

"No, but we don't want to wait until they get in position to blow up the chalet," Daphne reminded the men. "The sooner they think we're out of here, the better."

"You'll need snow pants, the protective vest and warm gloves." Boomer studied her. "Have you ever driven a snowmobile?"

She shook her head. "I'm good with the four-wheeler, but I don't have any experience on a snowmobile. Besides, I need to be on the back with my hair flying out for them to take the bait."

Boomer clenched his teeth. He didn't say anything for a moment or two. Using Daphne as bait to pull Cooper's cleanup team way from the chalet went against everything in his heart. But Daphne was adamant about getting them away from the house. With a sigh, he repeated his earlier order, "You'll ride with me."

"I'll be on the other vehicle to ride interference, should they get too close," Hank said.

Chuck held out his hands to Boomer. "And I'll be ready to take this little girl down the mountain when you get the bad guys away from here."

Boomer was reluctant to release Maya, but he did, a frown pulling his brow low. "I don't like leaving you alone with the baby."

Daphne slipped a hand into Boomer's. "Chuck will take care of Maya. He's her godfather."

"Damn right, I'll take care of her. She has a way of growing on you." Chuck smiled down at her and tickled her cheek.

Maya giggled and grabbed for Chuck's finger.

"I'll gather her things." Daphne hurried toward the bedroom.

"Put them in my truck," Hank said. "The one you came up in still has the trailer hitched to the bumper."

Daphne stuffed a bag full of diapers, warm clothing and the emergency can of formula powder. She draped baby blankets over the bag and hurried out into the living room. "We'll have to move the car seat into Hank's truck."

"I'll help with it," Boomer offered.

Daphne blinked, then gave a little smile of pleasure. "Thanks."

"We'll be back in a minute." Boomer held the door open.

Hank stepped through. "I'll stand watch while you take care of things." He carried the rifle he'd brought with him and took a position on the corner of the porch, staring out over the hillside sloping away from the house.

Boomer hooked Daphne's arm and hurried her out to the shed where they'd unloaded the two snowmobiles. The truck they'd brought them up on stood beside the shed, covered in twelve inches of snow.

"Stand between me and the shed."

She did as he said.

Still, Boomer shook his head. "I don't know why I let you talk me into this craziness."

"Because you know it's what we have to do if they come after us." She stared up at him. "We have to protect our baby."

Her bright green eyes captured his gaze for a moment, before his focus shifted to the soft rose of her lips. God, she was beautiful.

"I never stopped thinking of you after you disappeared." He pulled her into his arms. "Even in the desert, so far away from Cozumel. I remembered how your lips felt against mine."

She cupped his cheek. "I wanted to tell you where we'd gone, but it was too dangerous."

"We haven't seen each other in a year, but last night felt like we picked up where we left off. As if twelve months hadn't slipped away."

"Then why did you leave me?" she asked.

He pulled her close, crushing the bags between them, and lowered his head until his lips were a breath away from hers. "Because I'm an idiot. I don't want to fail you."

"The only way you'll fail me is if you push me away."

"I'm not the same man you met in Cozumel. There are things you don't know."

"You're right," Daphne said. "You aren't the same man. You're better. More mature, and even more handsome than before. So, shut up and kiss me. We don't have much time." She leaned up on her toes and pressed her lips to his.

Boomer clutched a handful of her hair and tugged, pulling her head back just a little. He crushed her lips with his, pushing his tongue past her teeth to slide along hers in a long, sensuous caress.

For a long moment, he held her like he should have the night before. When he came up for air, the whisper of a distant engine teased his ear.

His heart thudded. He lifted his head. "Do you hear that?"

She blinked open her eyes and tilted her head. "I do."

"We need to move. If they're on their way here, we have to be ready."

She nodded and hiked the diaper bag up on her arm. "It's time to get this show on the road."

Boomer knocked the snow off the roof and opened the back door. He unbuckled the car seat and backed out. As quickly as he could, he placed the baby's car seat in the back seat of Hank's truck and secured it. As he did, he prayed this insane plan would work, and Chuck would safely get Maya to that bunker in Hank's house. With Chuck watching out for Maya, Boomer would do his best to keep Daphne from becoming a sniper's target practice.

Chapter 9

As the engine sound grew louder, Daphne's pulse quickened. She tossed the diaper bag into the backseat and ran back to the house.

Boomer was right behind her, holding his rifle in his hands, not slung over his shoulder.

When Daphne burst through the door, Chuck and Hank stood.

"What's wrong?" Hank asked.

"We can hear the sound of engines," Daphne said.

"Engine or engines," Chuck asked.

"Engines," Boomer confirmed as he stepped up beside Daphne.

"Time to rock and roll." Hank tossed his truck keys to Chuck. "Hunker down until we get them to follow us, and then get Maya down the mountain."

Chuck held Maya in the crook of his arm. "Will do. For now, I'll take her into the back room in case there's any shooting."

Hank nodded and shrugged into his jacket. "Let's do this." He led the way out the door and to his truck where he pulled protective vests from the toolbox in the back. He handed one to Daphne and one to Boomer.

She shed her coat and slipped on the vest.

Then Hank reached in and pulled out a

small case, popped the latch on it and lifted a small handgun out of the foam padding. "Chuck assured me you know how to use one of these."

She nodded and took the weapon.

He handed her a belt with a black leather holster.

Daphne didn't ask questions. She wrapped the belt around her waist and hooked the buckle.

Then she donned her jacket, making sure the holster wasn't covered.

The engine sounds were getting closer. If they planned on getting out of there, they had to do it soon.

Boomer threw open the overhead door to the shed and straddled one of the snowmobiles. In seconds, he had the engine humming and pulled out onto the snow. He handed her a helmet.

Daphne pulled on the helmet, letting her long blond hair tumble down her back, in sharp contrast to the black jacket she wore. There would be no denying a blond female was on the back of the vehicle.

She climbed on the back and wrapped her arms around his waist. With a gun on her hip and a SEAL to hold onto, she felt unstoppable.

Hank climbed onto the other snowmobile and revved the engine. In the next moment, four snowmobiles appeared over the hilltop.

"There they are!' Daphne shouted over the roar of the motors.

"Hold on tight!" Boomer hit the throttle and

sent the snowmobile skidding around in a one-hundred-eighty-degree turn, heading past the house and up to the top of the ridge.

Daphne clung to Boomer's middle as her bottom slid sideways on the sharp turn. She tightened her arms around his middle. The only way she'd come off the seat of the snowmobile was if Boomer came off with her. She refused to slow them down.

The rear end of the snowmobile skidded to one side and then straightened, the tracks digging into the snow and gravel beneath, shooting them forward.

Hank took the rear position, covering them from behind. The plan was to split up and lead the cleanup team on a wild goose chase through the mountains. When they reached a decent position, Boomer and Hank would attempt to take them out before the bad guys had a chance to hurt them.

Daphne glanced over her shoulder, and her heartbeat rocketed.

The four snowmobiles raced toward them, flying up over bumps and across the rugged terrain.

Her grip tightened again as they topped the ridge on the other side of the chalet.

Boomer slowed long enough to make sure all four snowmobiles were following them.

Hank pulled up beside them and looked back.

The group of riders flew past the house and

followed their tracks up the side of the hill.

"Go!" Hank said.

Boomer gunned the accelerator, sending the snowmobile over the ridge and down a steep slope to the valley below.

Hank followed, paralleling them, but not so close that if he lost control he'd come crashing into them.

The four snowmobiles shot over the top of the ridge and plummeted toward the valley floor.

Daphne gasped.

The bad guys were traveling so fast that if they didn't slow, they'd either wreck at the bottom or overtake the two men and one woman before they had time to escape. Boomer's snowmobile was slower with two people on it. At the rate everyone was moving, it was only a matter of time before the gang following them caught up.

On the verge of second guessing her decision to use herself as bait, Daphne was surprised when Boomer topped a hill, rounded a bend in the terrain and climbed a steep incline, placing them on top of an overhang.

Hank spent a few precious minutes swishing a tree branch to cover their trail, and then took off on his snowmobile, laying down a fresh trail for their pursuers to follow.

Boomer shut down their engine, leaped off the seat and pulled out his rifle. "Stay down." He lay in the snow on the edge of the little cliff. Using the barrel of his rifle, he cleared a Vshaped wedge in the snow.

Daphne slipped off the snowmobile and dropped into the snow, low-crawling up to Boomer's left side.

They didn't speak, just waited.

Moments later, the four snowmobiles appeared.

Boomer's body tensed. He gripped his rifle in his hand, inhaled deeply and let the air out slowly, his eye trained on the scope.

"Do we know for sure these are the men who are after me?" Daphne asked.

"You want to walk down there and ask?"

She shook her head. "What if they're just recreational snowmobilers?"

Boomer's finger froze on the trigger.

As Daphne watched, the lead snowmobile came to a halt on the path below. The rider pulled off his goggles and motioned for the next man to move forward on his machine.

"You tell me. Is that Cooper or one of his hired guns?" Boomer leaned his head to the side "Look for yourself."

Daphne laid her cheek against his and stared down the scope. For a moment everything was blurred. Then she moved a little to the right and the images cleared.

The man who'd removed his goggles had dark hair and heavily tanned skin. He pulled a rifle from the scabbard on the side of the snowmobile and turned toward their position.

Daphne sucked in a sharp breath.

"Recognize him?" Boomer whispered.

Her heart pounded against her ribs. The man below her was one of the guys who'd swept in to carry off Cooper's kill in Cozumel.

Daphne leaned away from Boomer and pinched the bridge of her nose to keep from shouting out loud. "He's a member of the cleanup crew I saw in Cozumel."

The mercenary lifted the rifle to his shoulder. He stared into the scope and spun in a circle, searching his surroundings. The man slowed as he raised his rifle to the top of the hill where Boomer and Daphne perched on the edge of the cliff.

His eyes narrowed, and a loud bang echoed off the hillside.

The snow beside Daphne puffed upward, dusting her face.

Boomer laid a hand on her head and pushed her down.

Daphne gladly lay with her cheek in the cold, white snow, afraid to raise her head for fear of getting it blown off. She watched Boomer as he resumed his position, stared down the scope and squeezed the trigger.

Daphne gasped and shoved a fist into her mouth to keep from crying out, then couldn't resist taking a peek.

Below, the gunman staggered backward, clutching his chest.

One of the other men slid off his snowmobile and dropped behind it. The tip of a rifle appeared above the seat.

"Daphne, stay down," Boomer urged.

The crack of a rifle being fired split the snow-covered silence of the mountains.

Daphne hugged the earth, making a crater in the snow.

Engines revved and moved out.

Boomer trained his weapon on the movement below and fired off another round.

Daphne looked up long enough to see two snowmobiles race off. The man who'd been shooting at them lay on his back, a bright red stain in the snow surrounding his head.

Daphne's stomach roiled and she looked around. "Where did the other two riders go?"

"I don't know."

Her heartbeat quickened, and she came halfway up on her knees. "You don't think they went back to the chalet, do you?"

Boomer leaned dangerously close to the edge of the cliff.

Daphne grabbed a handful of his jacket to keep him from sliding off and crashing to the bottom a hundred feet down.

"Their tracks lead away from the house, but I'm hearing engine noise echoing off the hills. I can't tell where they're going." He scooted back from the drop-off and stood with his head tilted, a frown denting his brow. "Do you hear that?"

Daphne listened, her heart pounding against her ribs. The thumping sound of rotor blades whipping the air came to her over the hills.

"Helicopter," Boomer said.

"Good guys or bad guys?" Daphne asked.

He shook his head. "I don't know."

A shiver shook her from head to toe. "Do you think Chuck and Maya got away?"

"Only one way to know." He pulled her to her feet and into his arms. "We need to get back to the chalet."

She nodded, her gaze dropping to his lips. "Whatever happens between to the two of us, I want you to know, what we shared in Cozumel was the happiest time of my life."

His gaze darkened. "And mine." He lowered his head and captured her lips in a swift kiss that left her breathless and wanting so much more.

When Boomer raised his head, he touched a finger to her lips. "Hang onto that thought. I don't want to lose you again." He climbed onto the snowmobile.

Her heart surged with a rush of happiness. Boomer held out his arm to help her balance as she slipped on behind him, wrapped her arms around his waist and pressed her cheek to his back. Hope surged.

Just as Boomer started the engine, a single snowmobile appeared on the road below, followed by the two that had disappeared minutes before.

"Hank's in trouble," Boomer said.

Her heart banging against her ribs, Daphne leaned close to Boomer's ear to be heard over the sound of the engine. "We have to help."

Boomer's chest swelled.

The woman he'd fallen in love with on the resort island of Cozumel was brave and selfless. She'd sacrifice her own life for her daughter's, and she'd chase the enemy to save a friend.

She deserved a better man than him, but he wanted her and couldn't think of a future without her in it. And he wanted to get to know his baby girl. Maya looked like him. If her personality was anything like his, she'd be a handful. She needed someone who would understand her and help channel her energy and curiosity into something productive. Daphne would be patient and loving, the kind of mother any little girl could need.

Boomer shook his head to clear his thoughts. Right at the moment, he needed his wits about him, needed sharp focus to help Hank and keep Daphne from being hurt.

He raced down the side of the hill and followed the two snowmobiles gaining on Hank.

Hank veered his vehicle off the trail and climbed a hill. When he reached the top, he stopped suddenly. Then he raced his snowmobile across the ridgeline.

Why wasn't he going down the other side?

The two bad guys powered up the hill after him. Thankfully, the terrain demanded both hands on the handlebars to keep the snowmobile moving steadily forward. The riders couldn't pull out weapons to fire on Hank.

But as they climbed the hill after Hank, they were exposed and vulnerable.

Boomer brought the snowmobile to a halt.

"What are you doing?" Daphne shouted over the roar of the engine. "We have to help Hank."

Nodding, he shut off the engine, pulled his rifle from the sleeve he'd strapped to the snowmobile and rested the barrel across the handlebars.

Daphne slipped off the back of the snowmobile into a foot-and-a-half-deep snowdrift, giving Boomer more room to take aim.

He held steady, his sight trained on the snowmobile in the lead. When he was sure, he pulled the trigger.

The man on the vehicle in the lead jerked, and his hand flew into the air. The snowmobile turned, teetered and rolled sideways down the hill, throwing its rider in the process.

The second snowmobile spun and raced back down the hill, zigzagging, making the driver a more difficult target.

Boomer aimed, anticipating the next move and squeezed the trigger.

The driver jerked the handlebars. The snowmobile rocked up on one skid and dropped back to the earth, careening to the bottom of the hill where it crashed into a tree.

Hank turned his snowmobile and eased down the hillside.

Boomer trained his sights on the figure lying beside the crashed vehicle. The man moved, dragging himself through the snow toward what appeared to be a rifle that had been thrown ten feet from the crash site.

Fortunately, Hank reached the man before the man reached the rifle.

He kicked the rifle out of range of the man on the ground and pulled the man's arms behind him, securing them with a zip-tie.

"Hank has the last man secured." Boomer sat up on the snowmobile, sheathed the rifle in its scabbard and scooted forward making room for Daphne.

"Wow," she said, her voice soft and shaky. "You're really good with that rifle."

He turned to her, his brow descending as he studied her expression. "It was either them or us."

She nodded.

He waited, looking for her reaction and wondering if she could stomach this part of him.

"I know," she said softly. "I'm just glad you're with us." Daphne slid onto the seat behind him and wrapped her arms around him.

He liked the way it felt with her arms and legs pressed close. When they got back to Hank's house, he had to come to grips with his feelings for her and Maya and somehow convince himself and Daphne that he could be a part of their lives.

Boomer drove the snowmobile to where Hank had the man secured.

His boss had tended to a wound on the man's shoulder, packing it with fabric torn from the aggressor's T-shirt. Once he'd stemmed the flow of blood, he helped the man onto the back of his snowmobile, securing his wrists to the leather strap across the seat. "Let's see who we have here." He pulled off the man's helmet and glanced at Daphne. "Anyone you know?"

The injured man had dark hair and dark eyes. His face was pale from blood loss, and his head lolled a little, his eyes rolling as he tried to remain upright.

She shook her head. "Never saw him before now."

Hank snorted. "Another mercenary." He shoved the helmet back on his head and secured the strap. "We'll have to take it slow to get back to the chalet."

Boomer nodded. "You take the lead. If he falls off, I'll help you get him back on."

Hank eased the snowmobile up onto the trail, heading back the way they'd come. From the top of the ridge overlooking the chalet, Hank slowed and waited for Boomer to catch up. He removed his goggles and shot a glance at Boomer. "My truck is still there."

Boomer's gut clenched.

"What do you mean?" Daphne slid off the back of the snowmobile and stood looking down at the chalet. "Chuck and Maya should be halfway to your ranch." She grabbed the rifle from the scabbard.

Boomer reached out to take it, but she stepped out of reach.

"Hey, what are you doing?"

She squinted, staring through the scope. "Both trucks are still there."

Boomer laid his palm over the top of the rifle. Sighing she let him take it.

Hank dismounted from the snowmobile and walked several yards across the ridge to view the chalet from a different angle. He stopped suddenly and cursed.

"What?" Boomer asked.

"There's a helicopter parked in the clearing on the far side of the chalet." He shook his head. "What do you want to bet they've captured Chuck and Maya?"

Daphne gasped. "Maya." She took off running toward the trail leading down to the chalet.

Boomer caught up to her and then, holding the rifle away, he grabbed her arm and yanked her into his embrace. "What do you think you're going to do?"

She struggled against his hold. "Whatever it takes to free my baby."

"She's my baby, too. And running down there will only get you both killed."

"I can't let them hurt Maya." Daphne shook her head, tears streaming down her cheeks. "She's my life. She's all I have. I love her so much it hurts."

With his free arm, he pulled her more tightly

against his chest, trapping her arms against his body. "Sweetheart, she's mine, too. I promise you we'll get her back."

"Alive?" Daphne lifted her head and bit her lip. Tears dripped from her chin.

Her pain-filled glance tore at him. "Alive," he promised, though he wasn't sure how he'd accomplish that feat. "Right now, you're the only thing keeping them from hurting her. Maya's their leverage."

Hank returned to stand beside them. "He's right. They want you. To get you, they'll use whatever they can to lure you out into the open."

Daphne tried again to shake off Boomer's embrace. "Then let me go."

He shook his head. "If you go down there now, they'll shoot you. Once you're dead, they have no reason to keep Maya alive."

"But they want me, not Maya."

"They won't leave any of us alive," Hank said. "We'd be more witnesses to be disposed of."

"But we can't stand here and do nothing," she wailed, pushing at his chest. "There's no telling what they're doing to Maya, and to Chuck, for that matter."

Boomer's jaw tightened. "When I let go of you, can you promise me you won't run down there and get yourself shot?"

She bit her lip and stared into his eyes.

He squeezed her gently. "I promise I'll do everything in my power to save our daughter.

Promise me you won't run."

Slowly, she nodded her head. "Please save my baby."

"Our baby," he said, resting his forehead against hers. "I might not know how to take care of her like you and Chuck do, but I know I'll love her as much as you do. If you'll give me the chance to be with her and you."

"Yes!" Daphne said, her voice shaking. "Just save her. Please."

Boomer released Daphne, and with the rifle in his hands started across the ridge to where Hank stood. "We have to get in a position where we can see into the chalet. We need a headcount of the number of people holding them hostage."

Daphne followed. "How will that help?"

Boomer came to a halt when he faced the chalet's front porch and dropped to his belly in the snow. "We have to know how many people we're dealing with in order to make our move and not get Chuck or Maya kil—harmed."

Daphne stumbled, righted herself and dropped down beside Boomer.

Hank passed them, carrying another rifle with a scope. "I'll go a little farther along the ridge and let you know what I see."

Boomer nodded without saying a word. He concentrated all his focus on the door and windows to the chalet.

"What do you see?" Daphne asked.

"Not much. The shadow of the porch overhang keeps the doors and windows in the dark, and without the generator running, there are no lights on inside."

Daphne grabbed his arm. "Is the door opening?"

Boomer grimaced. "Sweetheart, don't touch, bump or nudge me while I have a rifle in my hands."

"I'm sorry, but look." She pointed. "Is that Chuck?"

Boomer had already ascertained the man who stepped out of the chalet was indeed Chuck. And he carried what appeared to be a bundle of baby blankets.

Daphne drew in a sharp breath. "Oh, my God. He has Maya, doesn't he?"

What Boomer could see through his scope that Daphne could not from this distance was the handgun pressed to the back of Chuck's head. If the gun went off and the bullet ricocheted inside the man's skull, there was no telling where it would exit, and whether it would hit Maya on the other side.

Boomer's palms sweated in the cold air.

"Daphne Miller!" a voice shouted from inside the chalet, the noise echoing off the hillsides. "If you want your daughter to live, come down now. You have exactly one minute before she dies."

Chapter 10

"Oh, sweet Jesus." Daphne struggled to her feet and started over the edge of the ridge. "I have to go."

Boomer dropped his rifle, snagged Daphne's hand and jerked her down beside him. His expression was taut with fury. "Don't you understand? If you go, they'll kill you."

Her heart thundered against her ribs. Her baby was down there with a psychopath. What did Boomer expect her to do? Stand by and let them kill an innocent child? "Better me than Maya," she said and struggled to free her wrist.

"You can't go." Still holding her wrist with one hand, he grabbed his rifle and fumbled with the clips holding the strap to the rifle's length.

Daphne braced her feet against the snow-covered, rocky terrain and pulled with all her might.

Boomer's grip was like an iron band. He refused to release her. When he'd freed the strap, he turned to her. "You're going to hate me for this, but I can't let you go down there. I risk losing you as well as Maya. I'm not willing to lose you both now that I've found you."

She stared down at the hand holding the strap. "What are you doing?"

He wrapped the strap around her wrists and dragged her backward, away from the edge of the ridge. "You have to stay put and let me do my job."

He looped the strap over a low-hanging tree branch and pulled it tight, knotting it snuggly.

"You can't leave me here." Daphne yanked and tugged, but his handiwork held. She wasn't going anywhere. "Damn it, Boomer, that's my baby down there. You can't keep me from her."

"I'm keeping you from getting yourself killed. Now, be quiet while Hank and I figure out how to handle this situation."

"One minute, Boomer," she whispered harshly. "A quarter of that is almost gone. You have to let me go down there." She pulled so hard, the strap rubbed her wrists raw. "Please, don't let my baby die." Tears ran down her cheeks.

Boomer resumed his position and stared through the scope. He lay for so long, without moving, Daphne thought he'd fallen asleep.

Please, don't shoot my baby. Please. She repeated the mantra beneath her breath, praying for a miracle.

Maya was not just the result of fling with a handsome SEAL on a resort island. She was the hope for the future Daphne had needed after losing her fiancé. She was the result of falling in love with a real hero. A man who'd suffered while defending their country and way of life. Maya was the glue that kept Daphne together and, hopefully, would bring and keep Boomer in their lives.

If Maya died...

More tears slipped down Daphne's cheeks. If Maya died, every happiness Daphne had dreamed of would be gone. She wasn't even sure she could be with Boomer knowing their baby was dead. Her baby looked like him. Seeing him every day would be a steady, painful reminder.

Anger replaced sadness. Anyone who could hold a baby hostage had to be the lowest form of life. He didn't deserve to live. Hell, she already knew that based on how he'd choked the life out of that woman in Cozumel. Harrison Cooper deserved to die.

"If you're going to shoot someone," Daphne shouted to Boomer, "make sure it's the bastards holding my baby hostage."

Boomer counted two people inside the chalet, besides Chuck and Maya.

After the man pointing the gun at Chuck's head had issued the ultimatum, he'd pulled Chuck and Maya back inside the building and closed the door.

"Ten seconds remaining," Hank called out. "I counted two men besides Chuck and Maya.

"I got the same," Boomer acknowledged.

"From where I am, I can take out the one further inside if you can take out the one who came to the door with Chuck."

"If they come out that way again, I can do it."

"Five seconds," Daphne said. "Please don't

hit Maya or Chuck. Anyone else if fair game."

Boomer's lips twitched. The woman had fight, and she would defend her child like a mother bear.

"Four...three...two...one..." Daphne whispered.

The door opened. Chuck stepped out onto the porch, holding Maya.

"Time's up!" the voice shouted.

Boomer could make out a blond-haired younger man holding a handgun to the back of Chuck's neck.

Chuck seemed to be saying something, but no sound was coming out of his mouth. He held Maya with two fingers pointing up.

Boomer concluded the man was confirming only two men were in the chalet.

Chuck leaned to one side slightly, giving Boomer a better line of sight at the man holding the gun.

He drew in a deep breath and held it, the crosshairs of his scope on the blond man's head. One slip-up, and he could kill Chuck or Maya.

Moisture gathered on his upper lip, and his finger curled around the trigger. Images of the Islamic State militant dressed in the white imam's robe rose up in Boomer's mind.

He blinked to clear the image and focused on the blond man, a far cry from the militant with the black hair and the black beard. He couldn't loose his concentration now. Not with his baby's life depending on him.

"You just sentenced your baby to death!" the man shouted.

"That man down there is not an ISIS militant. He's a murderer, and he's threatening our baby," Daphne whispered. "Shoot the bastard."

Boomer pulled himself out of the past and focused on his future. With the gentlest of pressure, he pulled the trigger.

The bullet blasted out of the rifle and a moment later hit the target.

Not even a second later, Hank fired a round, piercing the window of the chalet.

The blond man Boomer's bullet had struck jerked backward, and his gun went off. Chuck flinched and dropped to his knees, still holding the baby in his arms.

Boomer was on his feet and scrambling to release Daphne from the tree. He ran to the snowmobile and leaped onto the seat.

Daphne flung herself onto the back as Boomer revved the engine. Then they slipped and slid down the trail toward the chalet at breakneck speed.

When they came to a halt in front of the chalet, Boomer and Daphne flew off the snowmobile and ran toward the porch where Chuck sat, cradling Maya in his arms. Blood oozed from a wound on the side of his head, just above his ear.

Daphne dove for Maya and gathered the baby in her arms, peeling back the blankets to check for injuries.

"Maya's all right," Chuck said. "I made sure of it."

"Which is better than can be said for you," Boomer said quietly.

Chuck shook his head and winced. "He just nicked me."

Boomer knelt beside the blond man and felt for a pulse. There wasn't one.

"Harrison Cooper?" Boomer asked.

Chuck and Daphne nodded.

"He's dead." Boomer glanced across at Daphne. "He won't be bothering you or anyone else, ever again."

Daphne clutched Maya to her chest, her eyes narrowing. "Good. The bastard had it coming." She kissed Maya's forehead and wrapped her more tightly in the blanket.

Boomer moved into the chalet where he found a man dressed in a business suit lying on the floor, moaning, blood pooling beneath his shoulder.

Boomer stepped over the dead blond man "Who do we have here?"

"Harrison Cooper's father." Chuck had pushed to his feet and leaned against the doorframe. "Meet Senator John Cooper."

"You murdered my son," the man on the floor said through gritted teeth. "I'll have you all in the electric chair for what you've done."

"We think not," Boomer said. "Your days of killing off witnesses to your son's messes are over. The fact you're here, supported by a team of mercenaries, isn't going to look good to the authorities."

"You don't know what you're talking about," the senator said.

"The men you sent on snowmobiles to kill us didn't accomplish their mission."

"I suppose you killed them as well. The courts will see your actions as a brutal killing spree."

"The courts might have, but we saved one of your mercenaries," Boomer said. "My bet is he won't go down with you. I doubt you could pay him enough money to lie in front of judge and go to jail for you and your murdering son."

"It'll be my word against his—and yours."

"Not so fast, Senator." Chuck pulled a cell phone from his pocket. "I recorded everything— from your threats to your son's. We have multiple witnesses, including one of your own cleanup crew, who I'm sure will be eager to cut a sweet deal. You're going to jail, and your son's going to hell."

Several trucks appeared on the road leading up to the chalet. They were followed by a couple of county sheriff's vehicles.

Hank arrived on the porch, shoving the man from the snowmobile chase ahead of him. "The cavalry has arrived."

Boomer slipped an arm around Daphne. "We need to get Maya somewhere warm." With the door to the chalet wide open, and the generator turned off, the house would be as cold as the outside.

Daphne handed Maya to Boomer. "Take care of her while I help Chuck."

Boomer took Maya and tucked her, blanket and all, into his jacket.

Daphne took charge of tending to Chuck's "nick," cleaning the wound and wrapping his head in a swath of strips torn from a pillowcase.

With the bleeding stopped, Chuck smiled and hugged Daphne.

Boomer couldn't be angry with the man. He knew how it felt to be in love with Daphne, having loved her since they'd met in Cozumel.

Once law enforcement cleared them to leave after they'd promised to give their statements at the sheriff's office the following day, Boomer and Daphne took Maya and headed to the truck. They'd stay at Hank's ranch while Hank and Chuck remained behind to answer questions and make sure the senator didn't get away with his lies and treachery.

"Are you sure you don't want to wait for Chuck?" Boomer asked as he helped Daphne buckle Maya into the car seat.

She smiled over the top of Maya's head. "I love Chuck."

Boomer's heart plummeted into his belly, and he had a hard time concentrating on the multiple buckles that were part of the intricate car seat.

Daphne's grin broadened, and she reached

across Maya to touch Boomer's hand. "I love Chuck like a wonderful older brother. I don't know what I would have done without him this past year, and I want him to be a part of Maya's life." She squeezed his hand. "But you were what kept him at arm's length from me. Even when you were on the other side of the world, you were always in my heart and on my mind."

Boomer released a deep breath and stared across at her, sure she could see the moisture gathering in his eyes, but not giving a damn. He gave her a half-smile. "You don't know how happy that makes me. I'd hate to have duke it out with Chuck. Especially after he took such good care of our daughter." He lifted Daphne's hand to his lips and kissed her fingertips. "I love you Daphne Miller. I never stopped thinking about you. When I was up to my eyeballs in sandstorms and ISIS militants, I thought of you and how, when I got back to the States, I'd find you."

Her smile was sweet, her eyes misty. "And then you did."

"Thanks to Chuck and Hank," Boomer said. "Remind me to thank those two for bringing us back together." He backed out of the rear seat and closed the door. Before he could get around the truck to help Daphne into the passenger seat, she was already inside.

He'd have to step up his game if he wanted to show her how much she'd come to mean to him.

Chapter 11

Once he was behind the wheel of Hank's truck, Boomer eased down the road. The parade of trucks and sheriff's SUVs had packed the snow and made it easier to see the drop-offs. They made good time all the way back to the ranch.

When they pulled up in front of the sprawling ranch house, Boomer shifted into park, cut the engine and climbed down, hurrying around to Daphne's side. He opened the door and reached in, capturing her around the waist.

She laughed, the sound so much lighter and happier than he could remember. "I can get down from the truck myself."

"I know that. You're a very independent woman. Still…" He lifted her out of her seat and let her slide down his front until her feet touched the ground. "I like the way you feel against me."

"Mmm…you have a good point." She leaned up on her toes and pressed her lips to his. "And I like the way you taste."

He lowered his head and took her mouth in a crushing kiss. The sound of Maya stirring in the backseat brought him back to earth, reminding him they had responsibilities. "I'll bet she's hungry."

"Probably so." Daphne unbuckled the baby

from the car seat and carried her into house. She found a chair in the living room and settled down long enough to nurse Maya.

Boomer sat across from her. "Do you mind if I watch?"

Daphne shrugged. "Not at all."

He stared at the baby, suckling at her mother's breast. "Where did you get the name Maya?"

Daphne brushed a dark strand of Maya's hair back from her forehead. "Remember when you found me on the beach in Cozumel, on what was supposed to have been my honeymoon?"

He nodded. "You were sobbing buckets of tears. Seeing you like that nearly broke my heart."

Daphne smiled. "You were so good to listen to my sad story." Her smile faded. "Before Jonah died, he made me promise to go on the honeymoon and be open to love and life. Had he lived, we would have named our firstborn child after the resort where we were supposed to have shared on our honeymoon. So you see, you were not my first love." Daphne looked up into his face.

Boomer's brow twisted. "I'm not sure how I'm supposed to feel about that."

She smiled. "Good. I truly believe Jonah sent you to be with me in Cozumel. He was the guardian angel that led me to you." She held out her hand and took his in hers. "You might not have been my first love, but you are my last love and the father of our little girl."

"I will be sure to say a prayer for Jonah, thanking him for giving you to me and for the beautiful baby girl we have." He leaned over and kissed the baby's cheek. "Maya is a beautiful name for a beautiful little girl."

Daphne cupped his cheek. "You're not afraid of her anymore?"

"I was never afraid of Maya. I was more afraid I wouldn't be good enough for her."

"You're going to be a great father," Daphne said with a certainty Boomer wished he could feel.

"I hope so. One thing is for sure...I'm going to give it my best."

"That's all any parent can do." Daphne handed Maya to him. "You can start by learning to change her diaper. Then she'll need to be burped." Daphne winked. "Don't worry. You're going to be great."

Boomer laughed. "Yes, ma'am. I'd be honored." He gathered Maya in his arms and leaned over to press a kiss to Daphne's lips. "I love you Daphne Miller. And someday soon, I hope to marry you and Maya. You both mean so much to me."

Daphne's eyes widened. "Is that a proposal?"

He grinned. "Why yes. But if you want me to do a better job of it, I can do the whole down-on-a-knee thing." He started to get down on his knee, but Daphne stopped him by wrapping her arms around his neck, sandwiching Maya between them.

"You don't have to do that. My answer is

yes!"

Behind Boomer, a door opened and the clump of boots on the wooden floors heralded the entry of a number of men.

"Are we interrupting something?" Hank's voice called out. "We could go to the Blue Moose Tavern and have a drink or two and return later, if you like."

Boomer and Daphne turned to face Hank, Chuck and half a dozen of the Brotherhood Protectors.

Boomer laughed. "You don't have to leave. I'm betting you have beer and champagne somewhere in this big, beautiful house."

"Are we celebrating something?" Chuck asked, appearing like a wounded soldier with his head wrapped in white strips of fabric.

Boomer hooked his arm around Daphne's waist and hugged Maya with the other. "She said yes. Daphne, Maya and I are getting married."

Chuck's lips tightened for only a moment before he grinned. "About time. We can celebrate your engagement and Daphne's freedom from hiding."

"What happened to the senator?" Daphne asked.

"The sheriff hauled him off to jail."

"Who flew the helicopter?"

"Harrison Cooper had a pilot's license," Hank said. "His father was in the state campaigning for reelection. He flew him over to the chalet to witness what his money had bought in the way of mercenaries."

"Any chance the senator will be cleared of all charges?" Daphne asked.

Chuck shook his head. "No way. The hired gun was already asking for a plea bargain, claiming he'd spill his guts for a more lenient sentence."

Daphne sighed. "Then it's true? I'm free?"

Chuck nodded. "You're free."

She leaned into Boomer's side. "Then I can go shopping and not worry about being shot at."

Boomer laughed. "Yes, you can go shopping."

"Then tomorrow, I want to go to Bozeman to pick out my wedding dress." She stared up at Boomer. "You weren't kidding when you asked me to marry you, were you?"

He shook his head. "I want you in my life. I want to be there for you and Maya. The sooner the better."

She leaned up on her toes and kissed him. "Sooner, please."

Hank emerged from the kitchen, carrying glasses and a bottle of champagne. "If you prefer beer, there's a stash in the bar refrigerator."

Swede, Taz, Bear and Duke bypassed the champagne and went straight for the beer. Swede brought a longneck bottle to Boomer.

Daphne laughed and held up her hand to Hank. "You might as well put the champagne back in the fridge. I can't drink while I'm nursing, and I'm betting you'd rather have a beer."

Hank grinned. "You got that right."

Duke handed Hank a beer and all the men raised their bottles.

"To Daphne and Boomer!"

Boomer leaned down and kissed his bride-to-be. "Your strength makes me want to be a better man."

She cupped his cheek. "I love you, my Montana SEAL daddy."

About the Author

ELLE JAMES also writing as MYLA JACKSON is a *New York Times* and *USA Today* Bestselling author of books including cowboys, intrigues and paranormal adventures that keep her readers on the edges of their seats. With over eighty works in a variety of sub-genres and lengths she has published with Harlequin, Samhain, Ellora's Cave, Kensington, Cleis Press, and Avon. When she's not at her computer, she's traveling, snow skiing, boating, or riding her ATV, dreaming up new stories.

Learn more about Elle James at
www.ellejames.com

Or visit her alter ego Myla Jackson at
www.mylajackson.com

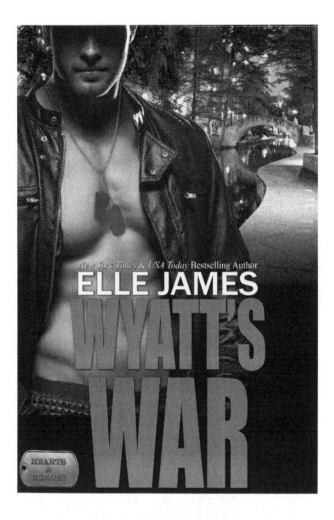

New York Times & USA Today Bestselling Author

ELLE JAMES

WYATT'S

WAR

WYATT'S WAR

Hearts & Heroes Series

Book #1

ELLE JAMES

New York Times & USA Today
Bestselling Author

Chapter One

Sergeant Major Wyatt Magnus pushed past the pain in his knee, forcing himself to finish a three-mile run in the sticky heat of south Texas. Thankfully his ribs had healed and his broken fingers had mended enough he could pull the trigger again. He didn't anticipate needing to use the nine-millimeter Beretta tucked beneath his fluorescent vest. San Antonio wasn't what he'd call a hot zone. Not like Somalia, his last *real* assignment.

It wouldn't be long before his commander saw he was fit for combat duty, not playing the role of a babysitter for fat tourists, politicians and businessmen visiting the Alamo and stuffing themselves on Tex-Mex food while pretending to attend an International Trade Convention.

The scents of fajitas and salsa filled the air, accompanied by the happy cadence of a mariachi band. Twinkle lights lit the trees along the downtown River Walk as he completed his run around the San Antonio Convention Center and started back to his hotel. Neither the food, nor the music lightened his spirits.

Since being medevaced out of Somalia to San Antonio Medical Center, the combined armed forces' medical facility, he'd been chomping at the bit to get back to where the action was. But for some damn reason, his commander and the psych evaluator thought he needed to cool his heels a little longer and get his head on straight before he went back into the more volatile situations.

So what? He'd been captured and tortured by Somali militants. If he hadn't been so trusting of the men he'd been sent to train in combat techniques, he might have picked up on the signs. Staff Sergeant Dane might not be dead and Wyatt wouldn't have spent three of the worst weeks of his life held captive. He'd been tortured: nine fingers, four ribs and one kneecap broken and had been beaten to within an inch of his life. All his training, his experience in the field, the culture briefings and in-country observations hadn't prepared him for complete betrayal by the very people he had been sent there to help.

He understood why the Somali armed forces had turned him over to the residual al-Shabab militants that were attempting a comeback after being ousted from the capital, Mogadishu. He might have done the same if his family had been kidnapped and threatened with torture and beheading if he didn't hand over the foreigners.

No, he'd have found a better way to deal with the terrorists. A way that involved very painful deaths. His breathing grew shallower and the beginning of a panic attack snuck up on him like a freight train.

Focus. The psych doc had given him methods to cope with the onset of anxiety that made him feel like he was having a heart attack. He had to focus to get his mind out of Somalia and torture and back to San Antonio and the River Walk.

Ahead he spied the pert twitch of a female butt encased in hot pink running shorts and a neon green tank top. Her ass was as far from the dry terrain of Somalia as a guy could get. Wyatt focused on her and her tight buttocks, picking up the pace to catch up. She was a pretty young woman with an MP3 device strapped to her arm with wires leading to the earbuds in her ears. Her dark red hair pulled back in a loose ponytail bounced with every step. Running in *the zone*, she seemed to ignore everything around but the path in front of her.

Once he caught up, Wyatt slowed to her pace, falling in behind. His heart rate slowed, returning to normal, his breathing regular and steady. Panic attack averted, he felt more normal, in control and aware of the time. As much as he liked following the pretty woman with the pink ass and the dark red, bobbing ponytail, he needed to get back and shower before he met the coordinator of the International Trade Convention.

Wyatt lengthened his stride and passed the woman, thankful that simply by jogging ahead of him, she'd brought him back to the present and out of a near clash with the crippling anxiety he refused to let get the better of him.

As he put distance between him and the woman in pink, he passed the shadow of a building. A movement out of the corner of his eye made him spin around. He jogged in a circle, his pulse ratcheting up, his body ready, instincts on high alert. The scuffle of feet made him circle again and stop. He crouched in a fighting stance and faced the threat, the memory of his abduction exploding in his mind, slamming him back to Somalia, back to the dry terrain of Africa and the twenty rebels who'd jumped him and Dane when they'd been leading a training exercise in the bush.

Instead of Somali militants garbed in camouflage and turbans, a small child darted out of his parents' reach and ran past Wyatt, headed toward the edge of the river.

His mother screamed, "Johnnie, stop!"

By the time Wyatt grasped that the child wasn't an al-Shabab fighter, the kid had nearly reached the edge.

Wyatt lunged for the boy and grabbed him by the scruff of the neck as the little guy tripped. Johnnie would have gone headfirst into the slow-moving, shallow water had Wyatt not snagged him at the last minute.

Instead of thanking Wyatt, the kid kicked, wiggled and squirmed until Wyatt was forced to set the boy on the ground. Then Johnnie planted the tip of his shoe in Wyatt's shin with razor-sharp precision.

Wyatt released him and bent to rub the sore spot.

Little Johnnie ran back to his mother, who wrapped her arms around the brat and cooed. Safe in his mother's arms, he glared at Wyatt.

Wyatt frowned, the ache in his shin nothing

compared to the way his heart raced all over again.

The boy's mother gave Wyatt an apologetic wince and hugged her baby boy to her chest. "Thank you."

A small crowd had gathered, more because Wyatt, the parents and child blocked the sidewalk than because they were interested in a man who'd just rescued a child from a potential drowning.

His heartbeat racing, his palms clammy and his pulse pounding so loudly in his ears he couldn't hear anything else, Wyatt nodded, glancing around for an escape. Fuck! What was wrong with him? If he didn't get away quickly, he'd succumb this time. Where was the woman in the pink shorts when he needed her? Some of his panic attacks had been so intense he'd actually thought he was having a heart attack. He hadn't told his commander, or the psychologist assigned to his case, for fear of setting back his reassignment even further. He wanted to be back in the field where the action was. Where he was fighting a real enemy, not himself.

As it was, he'd been given this snowbird task of heading up the security for the International Trade Convention. "Do this job, prove you're one hundred percent and we'll take it from there," Captain Ketchum had said. To Wyatt, it sounded like a load of bullshit with no promises.

Hell, any trained monkey could provide security for a bunch of businessmen. What did Ketchum think Wyatt could add to the professional security firm hired to man the exits and provide a visual deterrent to pickpockets and vagrants?

Wyatt had tried to see the assignment from his commander's point of view. He was a soldier barely recovered from a shitload of injuries caused by violent militants who set no value on life, limb and liberty. Sure, he'd been so close to death he almost prayed for it, but he was back as good as—

A twinge in his knee, made it buckle. Rather than fall in front of all those people, Wyatt swung around like he meant it and stepped out smartly.

And barreled into the woman he'd been following. Her head down, intent on moving, she'd been squeezing past him at that exact moment.

The female staggered sideways, her hands flailing in the air as she reached out to grab something to hold onto. When her fingers only met air, she toppled over the edge and fell into the river with a huge splash.

Another lady screamed and the crowd that had been standing on the sidewalk rushed to the edge of the river, pushing Wyatt forward to the point he almost went in with the woman.

A dark, wet head rose from the water like an avenging Titan, spewing curses. She pushed lank strands of hair from her face and glared up at him. "Are you just going to stand there and stare? Or are you going to get me out of this?"

Guilt and the gentleman in Wyatt urged him

to hold out his hand to her. She grasped it firmly and held on as he pulled her out of the river and onto the sidewalk. She was so light, he yanked with more force than necessary and she fell against him, her tight little wet body pressing against his.

His arm rose to her waist automatically, holding her close until she was steady on her own feet.

The redhead stared up into his eyes, her own green ones wide, sparkling with anger, her pretty little mouth shaped in an O.

At this close range, Wyatt saw the freckles sprinkled across her nose. Instead of making her face appear flawed, they added to her beauty, making her more approachable, though not quite girl-next-door. She was entirely too sexy for that moniker. Especially all wet with her skin showing through the thin fabric of the lime green tank top.

Then she was pushing against him—all business and righteous anger.

A round of applause sounded behind him, though he didn't deserve it since he'd knocked her into the water in the first place. "My apologies, darlin'."

She fished the MP3 out of the strap around her arm and pressed the buttons on it, shaking her head. "Well, that one's toast."

"Sweetheart, I'll buy you a new one," Wyatt said, giving her his most charming smile. "Just give me your name and number so that I can find you to replace it."

"No thanks. I'm not your sweetheart and I don't have time to deal with it." She squeezed the water out of her hair and turned away, dropping the MP3 into a trashcan.

With her body shape imprinted in dank river water on his vest and PT shorts, he was reluctant to let her leave without finding out her name. "At least let me know your name."

She hesitated, opened her mouth to say something, then she shook her head as if thinking better of it. "Sorry, I've gotta go." She shrugged free of his grip and took off, disappearing into the throng of tourists on the River Walk.

Wyatt would have jogged after her, but the number of people on the sidewalk made it impossible for a big guy like him to ease his way through. Regret tugged at his gut. Although he hadn't made the best first impression on her, her bright green eyes and tight little body had given him the first twinge of lust he'd felt since he'd been in Somalia. Perhaps being on snowbird detail would help him get his mojo back. At the very least, he might find time, and a willing woman, to get laid. Okay, so a few days of R&R in a cushy assignment might not be too bad.

A flash of pretty green eyes haunted his every step as he wove his way through the thickening crowd to his hotel where he'd stashed his duffel bag. He wondered if in an entire city of people he'd manage to run into the red-haired jogger again. If so, maybe he could refrain from knocking her into the river next time and instead get her number.

Fiona Allen arrived at the door to her hotel room, dripping wet and in need of a shower to rinse off the not-so-sanitary San Antonio River water. She couldn't afford to come down with some disease this week. Not when dignitaries were already arriving for the International Trade Convention due to kick off in less than two days' time.

If she did come down with something, it would all be that big, hulking, decidedly sexy, beast of a man's fault. The one who'd knocked her into the river in the first place. When he'd pulled her out with one hand, he'd barely strained.

Her heart had raced when he'd slammed her up against his chest. She blamed it on the shock of being thrown into the river, but she suspected the solid wall of muscles she'd rested her hands against had more to do with it.

For a brief moment, she'd remained dumbstruck and utterly attracted to the clumsy stranger. Had it been any other circumstance and she hadn't been covered in river slime, she might have asked for his number. *Yeah, right.*

As the convention coordinator, she couldn't afford to date or be sick, or for anything to go wrong while thousands of businessmen and politicians attended the meetings. She'd been hired by the city to ensure this event went off without a hitch, and she wouldn't let a single disgruntled employee, terrorist or hulking bodybuilder knock her off her game. No sir. She had all the plans locked up tighter than Fort Knox and the hired staff marching to the beat of her military-style drum.

She wasn't the daughter of an Army colonel for nothing. She knew discipline; hard work and using your brain couldn't be replaced by help from sexy strangers with insincere apologies. If this convention was going to be a success, it would be so based on all of her hard work in the planning stages.

Once inside her room, she headed straight for the bathroom and twisted the knob on the shower, amazed at how much her breasts still tingled after being smashed against the broad chest of the clumsy oaf who'd knocked her into the river. She shook her head, attributing the tingling to the chill of the air conditioning unit.

In the bathroom, she stripped her damp gym shorts and tank top, dropping the soaked mess into a plastic bag. She'd hand it over to the hotel staff and ask them to launder them, otherwise she'd have nothing to work out in. Who was she kidding? She wouldn't need to work out once the convention began.

Fiona unclipped her bra and slid out of her panties, adding them to the bag of dirty clothes. Then she stepped beneath the shower's spray and attacked her body with shampoo and citrus-scented soap. Images of the muscle man on the River Walk resurfaced, teasing her body into a lather that had nothing to do with the bar of soap. Too bad her time wasn't her own. The man had certainly piqued her interest. Not that she'd find him again in a city of over a million people.

As she slid her soap-covered hand over her breast, she paused to tweak a nipple and moaned. It had been far too long since she'd been with a man. She'd have to do something about that soon. With her, a little sex went a long way. Perhaps she would test the batteries in her vibrator and make do with pleasuring herself. Although the device was cold and couldn't give her all she wanted, it was a lot less messy in so very many ways. Relationships required work. Building a business had taken all of her time.

Fiona trailed her hand down her belly to the tuft of curls over her mons and sighed. Maybe she'd find a man. After the convention when her life wasn't nearly as crazy. She rinsed, switched off the water and stepped out on the mat, her core pulsing, her clit throbbing, needy and unfulfilled.

With a lot of items still begging for her attention, she couldn't afford the luxury of standing beneath the hot spray of the massaging showerhead, masturbating. Towel in hand, she rubbed her skin briskly, her breasts tingling at the thought of the big guy on the River Walk.

By the time the convention was over, that man could be long gone. He probably was a businessman passing through, or one of the military men on temporary duty. Even if he lived in the city, what were the chances of running into him again? Slim to none. San Antonio was a big place with a lot of people.

Well, damn. She should have given him her name and number. A quick fling would get her over her lust cravings and back to her laser-sharp focus.

She dragged a brush through her long, curly hair, wishing she'd cut it all off. With the convention taking all of her spare time, she didn't have time to waste on taming her mane of cursed curls. Most of the time it was the bane of her existence, requiring almost an hour of steady work with the straightener to pull the curls out. Having left her clean clothes in the drawer in the bedroom, Fiona stood naked in front of the mirror as she blew her hair dry, coaxing it around a large round brush.

This convention was her shot at taking her business international. If she succeeded and pulled off the biggest event of her career without a hitch, other jobs would come her way on her own merit, not based on a recommendation from one of her stepfather's cronies.

When she'd graduated with her masters in Operations Management, she'd invested the money her mother had left her in her business, F.A. International Event Planner. Since then, she'd steadily built her client list from companies based in San Antonio. Starting out with weddings, parties and small gigs, she'd established a reputation for attention to detail and an ability to follow through. She'd worked her way in as a consultant for some of the larger firms in the area when they'd needed to plan a convention based in San Antonio.

Finally she'd gotten a lead on the International Trade Convention and had applied. Her stepfather put a bug in the ear of one of his buddies from his active Army days at the Pentagon and she'd landed the contract.

Now all she had to do was prove she was up to the task. If it fell apart, she'd lose her business, disgrace the U.S. government and shame her stepfather. The pressure to succeed had almost been overwhelming. To manage the workload, she'd taken out a big loan, more than doubled her staff, coordinated the use of the convention center, arranged for all the food, meeting rooms, audio-visual equipment, translators, and blocked out lodging and security for the guests.

As she dried her hair, she stared at the shadows beneath her eyes. Only a few more sleepless nights and the convention would be underway and over. She'd be playing the role of orchestra conductor, managing the staff to ensure everything was perfect. The most important aspect of the event was tight security. The Department of Homeland Security had notified her today that with all the foreign delegates scheduled to attend, the probability of a terrorist attack had risen to threat level orange.

A quick glance at her watch reminded her that she only had ten minutes to get ready before her meeting in the lounge with the man

Homeland Security had insisted she add to her staff to oversee security. This last-minute addition made her nervous. She knew nothing about the man, his background or his capabilities. He could prove more of a hindrance than a help if he got in the way. All she knew was that he'd better be on time, and he'd better be good. With a hundred items roiling around in her head at any one moment, the last thing she needed was an international incident.

Fiona shut off the blow dryer, ran the brush through her hair and reached for the doorknob, reminding herself to look at the e-mail on her laptop from Homeland Security to get the name of the contact she'd be meeting shortly. Before she could turn the doorknob, it twisted in her hand and the door flew open.

A very naked man, with wild eyes and bared teeth shoved her up against the wall, pinned her wrists above her head and demanded, "Who the hell are you? And why are you in my room?"

Other Titles
by Elle James

Brotherhood Protectors Series
Montana SEAL (#1)
Bride Protector SEAL (#2)
Montana D-Force (#3)
Cowboy D-Force (#4)
Montana Ranger (#5)
Montana Dog Soldier (#6)
Montana SEAL Daddy (#7)
Montana Rescue (#8)

Take No Prisoners Series
SEAL's Honor (#1)
SEAL's Ultimate Challenge (#1.5)
SEAL's Desire (#2)
SEAL's Embrace (#3)
SEAL's Obsession (#4)
SEAL's Proposal (#5)
SEAL's Seduction (#6)
SEAL's Defiance (#7)
SEAL's Deception (#8)
SEAL's Deliverance (#9)

Hearts & Heroes Series
Wyatt's War (#1)
Mack's Witness (#2)
Ronin's Return (#3)
Sam's Surrender (#4)

Cowboy Brigade
Time Raiders: The Whisper
Bundle of Trouble
Killer Body
Operation XOXO
An Unexpected Clue
Baby Bling
Nick of Time
Under Suspicion, With Child
Texas-Sized Secrets
Alaskan Fantasy
Blown Away
Cowboy Sanctuary
Lakota Baby
Dakota Meltdown
Beneath the Texas Moon

66476409R00111

Made in the USA
Lexington, KY
15 August 2017